THE Treehouse

ETHAN A. WOHLWEND

The Treehouse

Quantity sales special discounts are available on quantity purchases by corporations, associations, and others. For details, contact the publisher at info@labricollective.com

Orders by U.S. trade bookstores and wholesalers.
Email: info@labricollective.com

Creative contribution by Mike Vreeland
Cover Design - Low & Joe Creative, Brea, CA 92821
Illustrations - Pat Byrnes
Book Layout - DBree, StoneBear Design

Manufactured and printed in the United States of America distributed globally by markvictorhansenlibrary.com

MVHL

New York | Los Angeles | London | Sydney

ISBN: 979-8-88581-069-2 Hardback
ISBN: 979-8-88581-070-8 Paperback
ISBN: 979-8-88581-075-3 eBook
Library of Congress Control Number: 2022920023

CONTENTS

1

ON THE LOOSE

arius was at his bedroom desk, absorbed in a Google search when he felt a slight breeze waft past him. The hairs on the back of his neck stood up. He looked out the open window at the quiet backyard. Not a leaf was moving in the heat of the June afternoon. He looked at his hamster's empty cage. His younger brother, Paulie, must have Harold out playing in his hamster ball. Darius focused back on his work.

A slight creak sounded behind him. He looked up from his computer screen and turned in his chair.

"Hey, Paulie, why are you sneaking into the room? It's your room, too."

"It's not that. It's Harold. He got out of his ball."

"Again?"

"I didn't want to tell you because I knew you'd be upset. I tried to find him myself, but I can't."

"You need to make sure the door in his ball is secured tightly every time."

Darius followed his brother downstairs to the living room. Paulie looked like a mini version of Darius, except that his curly mop of hair was blond and not dark brown.

The empty plastic ball sat on the floor next to the sofa. Darius scanned the room. No sign of Harold.

"How long has he been out?" asked Darius.

"Not too long."

"What does that mean, exactly?"

Paulie sighed. "Harold was having fun rolling around, and I started to read this magazine and then I didn't hear Harold rolling. When I checked, the ball was empty. Maybe five minutes. Ten? I'm not sure."

"Paulie. You need to pay more attention to detail."

"I know. I know. You sound like Mom and Dad."

"Well?" Darius and his brother usually got along great, but sometimes a nine-year-old can be exasperating to an almost thirteen-year-old. "You start over by the recliners. I'll start over here."

Darius peered under the sofa, then took out his phone, turned on its flashlight, and checked again. "Not here."

"Not here either," said Paulie, sitting on the floor.

"Don't stop looking," Darius prodded. "He's not going to walk out and say hello."

"I wish he would. A talking hamster. We'd make millions."

"There you go again. Focus." Darius crept along the floor and moved the drapes. Still, no Harold.

The boys spent several more minutes looking in the living room, dining room, and kitchen, anywhere Harold could have wandered off to, but Harold was nowhere. The doors to the other downstairs rooms were closed.

"He couldn't have climbed the stairs, could he?" asked Paulie.

"I don't think he could jump high enough to reach the next step," Darius replied.

Their mother opened the door from the basement and stepped into the kitchen with a basket of clean laundry.

"What's up, you two?" she asked.

"Harold is missing," Paulie said.

"Again," added Darius. "Paulie wasn't paying attention to him in his ball."

Paulie looked at the floor.

Everywhere their mother asked about, they had already checked.

Darius had an idea. "Maybe Harold sneaked into the basement when you went down before."

"I did leave the door open when I was carrying the laundry down. It would have been open for a few minutes while I was downstairs." She looked toward the basement door.

Darius continued, "And I know Harold can go

down steps. He just flops from one to the next. I've seen him. Kind of like a furry Slinky."

The boys headed down the stairs. Darius looked at the expanse of the basement.

"Harold could be anywhere. You start by the washer and dryer," he told Paulie, "I'll check by the furnace and water heater."

For the next several minutes, the boys made their way around the basement, looking behind plastic totes of holiday decorations, camping equipment, toys, and tools.

They scanned corners and every space large enough for Harold to squeeze into.

They sat on their father's home gym bench; shoulders slumped.

"Now what?" asked Paulie. "He's not down here."

"We didn't find him. That doesn't mean he's not down here. It just means we didn't find him."

"But we could be looking all day," Paulie whined.

"You were the one who let him escape," Darius pointed out. "No complaining from you."

Paulie sat up. "Maybe he'll come out when he's hungry."

Darius had an idea. "Maybe we can lure him out with some food."

"But we don't know where he is."

"We can leave bits of food in a few places. Every little while, we can check. If food is missing, we'll know where he is."

"Or was," said Paulie.

"True, but it's a start."

The boys set about leaving three pieces of food in several locations in the basement and in the living room, dining room, and kitchen. Darius set his phone alarm to sound every fifteen minutes.

***

The fifteen-minute checks continued all afternoon and during dinner.

"We're not having much luck," Darius admitted. "I hope he's not stuck somewhere."

His father was more optimistic. "Harold will turn up, I'm sure."

Darius tried not to think of anything bad happening to Harold. He didn't want to be mad at his brother, but he could feel his anger building the longer Harold was missing. He kept telling himself that Paulie didn't lose Harold on purpose, and that kept him focused on finding Harold instead.

Paulie was unusually quiet at the table. "I'll go," he said, jumping up when the alarm went off.

While he was down in the basement, Darius asked

his parents, "I know Paulie didn't mean it, but he's done this before. Can I tell him he can't play with Harold anymore?

"He loves Harold," Darius's mother said.

"I know, but–"

"You and Paulie need to negotiate something that works for you both."

Paulie returned from the basement. He shook his head and sat in his seat.

Darius could see Paulie's eyes welling up as he resumed eating his spaghetti.

Later that evening, Darius and Paulie were sitting on the sofa watching a documentary about Jane Goodall and her work with chimpanzees when Darius's alarm went off. He put the show on pause.

The boys got up from the sofa.

"Look," shouted Paulie. "A piece of food is missing. Harold was here by our feet while we were watching the show."

"Okay, at least we can stop looking in the basement," said Darius. "Running up and down the stairs was getting tiring."

"But where is he hiding?" asked Paulie.

"I think he's hiding up inside the sofa."

"You mean we've been sitting on him this whole time?"

"Probably."

Their father came into the living room to see what the commotion was.

Darius explained the situation.

"Let's open the sofa and take a look," said their father.

"Open the sofa?" Paulie asked.

"It's a sofa bed. It opens into a bed. Don't you remember when your Aunt Ellen and Uncle Pete came to visit?"

"Yeah, but I don't remember a bed."

Under the direction of their father, the three of them opened the bed while keeping watch for Harold.

Harold sat up as the bed opened, a piece of half-eaten hamster food next to him.

"There you are," exclaimed Darius, scooping him up and heading straight up the stairs to return him to his cage.

By the time Darius returned to the living room, Paulie had picked up the piles of food from around the house.

The boys sat back down on the sofa and returned to watching the documentary. Darius noticed the chimpanzees high in the trees looking out over the land below them. He wondered if they admired the view or if they just climbed the trees for safety. Darius

liked climbing trees for the views, but sitting on the branches would get quite uncomfortable in minutes. The chimpanzees, he noticed, didn't sit still for long. Maybe that's the secret, he thought.

A few minutes later, the alarm sounded again, and they both jumped up, ready to check for Harold.

They looked at each other and laughed.

"I guess I'd better turn that off or we'll be up all night," said Darius.

"I'm just glad we found Harold," Paulie said.

"About that. We need to talk."

2

NEW INSIGHTS

arius heard his phone ping. A triple question mark text from his friend, Katie. That was their code to call instead of text. He dialed her number.

"What's up, Katie?"

"Do you want to ride down to Happy Lake and hit up the library this afternoon? I need to pick up books from my reading list. Not too early to get started on required summer reading."

"It's not even summer yet," Darius protested, "but I'll ride down with you if my mom says it's okay. I'll text you after I ask her. Is your brother coming, too?"

"No, he says libraries are boring. I think he's just saying that because he hates the trip back home from Happy Lake. All uphill. If he would learn how to shift gears better, he wouldn't complain so much."

"That's what he gets for spending all his free time playing video games. Soggy muscles."

***

After a quick lunch of a peanut butter, potato chip, and banana sandwich, and a glass of chocolate milk, Darius jumped on his bike and headed toward Katie's

house. Even though Darius lived nearest to Rocky Point in an area known as Hilltop Meadows, he was only a couple of miles above Happy Lake, a lakeside community known for its little shops and over-the-top holiday events. On Darius's road, houses were far apart with fields and woodlands here and there, reminders it was once farmland.

His nearest neighbor was Mr. Wilson, a longtime friend of Darius's family. Darius waved at Mr. Wilson sitting on his front porch as he rode past. Since he retired a few years ago, Mr. Wilson spent most warm afternoons on his porch reading and, as he is fond of saying, watching the world go by.

Mr. Wilson's little dog ran out, yipping a friendly greeting.

"Hello, Champ," Darius called. He stopped and leaned down to pet the little cream-colored dog. "Gotta go, Champ." Champ tried to follow him even as Mr. Wilson called his name. Darius pedaled faster to outrun Champ until the dog gave up and turned for home. Once in the clear, Darius coasted downhill, around a corner, and into Katie's driveway.

Katie was on her bike already, and the two set off for the Happy Lake Public Library.

In minutes, they were pedaling along Main Street.

"Well, if it isn't my two favorite bibliophiles," said

the smiling librarian as he stood up from his stool behind the front desk when they entered. "What are we looking for today?"

"What's a bibliophile?" asked Darius.

"A lover of books," replied the librarian. "And you two are here often enough, you must love books."

"I'm here to start on my required summer reading list," added Katie. She held up her phone, showing him the list.

"Ooh, I despise the word required," he said. "I prefer to think of it as an unknown adventure that's been recommended to me."

"You make it sound fun."

"There is a reason those books are classics. A bibliophile like yourself will enjoy them for sure. Most of these are on the far shelf under the window."

It only took Katie a couple of minutes to find what she needed. She checked out the books and thanked the librarian.

Once outside, Katie placed the books in her bike basket. "We have time to stop for an ice cream."

"I don't have any money on me," Darius said.

"And what I have, I'm trying to save up for some really nice headphones."

"I only have two dollars on me. Maybe next time."

"I need to find a way to earn some money."

"I've been babysitting my neighbors' two little kids."

"Babysitting isn't going to do it for me. I have enough of little kids with Paulie."

"Aw. He's so cute."

"Most of the time, but not when he wants to play and I'm in the middle of something. Or when he loses Harold."

"Again?"

"Yes. But we found him." Darius confided in Katie, "Sometimes I wish I had a space of my own."

"I know what you mean. At least I have my own room, except when my stepdad's kids visit."

"I would have my own room, but my mom is using the other bedroom for her home office."

Darius rode behind Katie, looking at the shops, but thinking about his desire for a space all his own.

They decided to take a longer route home, one where the roads were not as steep.

As they left the downtown area, Darius noticed two boys pulling carts behind their bikes along one of the side streets. Each cart held a lawnmower. The boys must have seen Darius and Katie looking, because they waved as they passed on the opposite side of the street.

"Cool carts," Darius called.

"Thanks," one of the boys hollered back.

Darius studied the carts until the boys were too far away to see. The carts looked like they were made from wire crates and bicycle wheels attached to an axle. *Simple, but awesome*, Darius thought.

"You should get one of those carts for all the books you take out, Katie," Darius teased.

Katie didn't realize it was a tease. "It would mean fewer trips I'd have to make to the library, for sure."

They turned the corner, going faster on the flat stretch of road.

Darius commented, "I don't know why your brother thinks it's all uphill. There are plenty of flat spots."

"Soggy muscles, remember?"

About halfway home, the two slowed down as a construction site came into view. A dirt driveway led up to a concrete foundation. Several workers were nailing together wood framing for walls.

"Looks like a new house going up," Darius said.

"And a big one at that," Katie replied.

They stopped to survey the scene and watch the workers. The sounds of power saws and nail guns filled the afternoon air. Another section of wall framing was lifted into place and workers moved to secure it.

"That's some great teamwork," Darius commented.

Katie nodded. "That's how they can work so fast, I'll bet."

Darius noticed a chain-link fence surrounded the property. Along the fence at eye level were warning signs and private property signs. Just inside the fence near the driveway, Darius spied a pile of scrap wood. An idea crept into his mind. *I could build something with that wood.*

3

SCRAP TO TREASURE

arius waved toward the workers. They waved back. He wanted to ask about the wood, but they just returned to their work. He hopped off his bike and leaned it against the fence.

"Hello," he called. "Is this scrap wood, or do you still need it?"

One of the workers, a big beefy guy in jeans, a sleeveless orange shirt, and a yellow hard hat, walked down the long driveway toward them.

"Sorry to bother you," Darius continued, "but I was wondering if this wood is being thrown away."

"It is. You want it? You can have it. Save me from having to get rid of it."

"Really? Thanks." Darius was quick to make his way to the pile. Katie followed. They sorted through the pile and examined the wood.

"I don't know how much of it you can get on your bikes, but you can try," said the man. He pulled a handkerchief from his back pocket and wiped the sweat from his forehead.

"We don't live too far from here. We can make another trip," Darius said, hoping that would be okay.

"Don't take anything if we're not here working. I wouldn't want you getting in trouble."

"Trouble?" asked Katie.

"Somebody might think you are stealing it."

"That wouldn't be good, for sure," Katie replied, laughing.

"We're here every day until five, except on weekends."

Darius's eyes widened. "You mean there will be more wood?"

"More than likely. We toss all the bracing once we're done with it. And the odd lengths of ends. Help yourself. Just be careful. Splinters hurt."

With that, the man walked back up the driveway and left them to sort through the pieces.

There were a few two-by-fours, some long, some short, the ends of two-by-twelves cut at various angles, and smaller sizes of several lengths. Most looked used.

"Why are these so dirty?' Katie asked, pointing to a few with grey streaks and lumps.

"They were probably used for the basement to make a form when they poured the concrete. That can be washed off, I hope."

"What are you going to do with this wood once you get it home?" Katie asked.

"Not sure yet. Maybe build a fort or something if I get enough wood."

Darius looked at three large pieces of plywood. "I have to figure out a way to get those home."

"You'll think of something," Katie assured him. "Aren't you always the one saying not to say I can't?"

"But I didn't say it."

"Don't get technical. If you want the wood, you'll find a way."

Darius knew she was right. He was not one to give up on things.

They started down the road with their loads.

After a couple of minutes of struggling, Darius admitted, "We need a better way to do this." He stopped again to pick up the boards that had fallen from his handlebars.

"Rope would help," Katie offered. "Maybe we should leave them hidden in the weeds and come back with some rope."

"Good idea."

They tossed the boards into tall weeds on the side of the road and hurried off to Darius's house.

***

As they rounded a corner on their way back, they stopped. In the distance, at the spot where they had

left the boards, they saw a man standing next to his bike looking into the weeds.

"Uh, oh," said Katie. "What now?"

"Let's see what he wants." Darius's heart was pounding, but he wanted those boards more than he feared confrontation.

As they rode closer, Darius realized the man was actually a boy not much older than themselves. He was bigger and muscular with short, slicked back hair and tanned skin.

"Is this stuff yours?" the boy asked pointing into the weeds as they hopped off and walked their bikes over to him.

"Yes," Darius answered. "We left it here to get some rope to tie them to our bikes."

The boy straddled his bike as if preparing to leave and watched as they pulled the boards out of the weeds and set about arranging them into two stacks.

"You're good with knots," the boy commented.

"Boy Scouts," Darius answered. He lifted one of the stacks to set on Katie's basket, but its uneven weight caused him to lose his balance.

"Here. Let me help," said the boy, hopping off his bike and grabbing one end of the stack.

"Thanks. I'm Darius, and this is Katie."

"I'm Joe."

"That's a nice bike, Joe," Katie said.

"It's not mine. It's Coach's. He wants me to ride at least ten miles a day to build up my leg muscles some more."

Darius looked at Joe's bulging thigh muscles and couldn't imagine Joe needing to build up more muscle. "What sport? Track?"

"No, baseball. But my favorite is football. In the winter I play basketball, and in the spring, I play baseball. You play?"

"Not on a team, but I play baseball with friends."

Katie added, "I play soccer on an AYSO team. We're not very good, but it's fun and I get exercise."

"There's not much point if it's not fun," Joe agreed.

Darius finished tying the boards across Katie's basket while she held the bike steady. Then the two boys tied the second stack across Darius's handlebars.

"Nice meeting you, Joe," Katie said.

"Same," said Joe. "What you guys need is a cart. I saw this guy pulling a cart behind his bike down in Happy Lake. He had a lawn mower in it. It looked like it was made of old bike wheels and a metal frame. Kind of cool, actually."

"We saw it, too. There were two of them," Darius said. He tried to picture carrying wood in a cart like the ones he saw. *It would definitely need some modifications.*

Joe took off down the road in the opposite direction. Darius and Katie inched along with their wide wobbly loads, ready to stop and turn their handlebars sideways if a car should come along.

***

The following morning, Darius rushed through his studies to finish working on his wood carting idea.

"What do you think?" Darius asked Katie as she brought her bike to a stop in his driveway that afternoon.

"It's not a cart, but it looks like it will work."

"I didn't have any wheels. And then I thought about how long a cart would have to be to haul boards behind the bike. And how would they balance? And how would I turn corners? It was getting too complicated. I've been testing this out since last night. I mounted a piece of board sticking out behind the bike seat on either side, the same width as the handlebars. The bungee cords attached to it will hold the boards up in the back, and the bungee cords in the front let the boards hang off the handlebars. I can still steer. The only thing is the weight of the boards has to be the same on both sides of the bike or it's hard to keep your balance."

"This is great. Can you do the same for my bike?"

"Sure, but maybe we should test this out on a real load on the road first. You can be the backup in case it doesn't work."

Darius took the test boards off and set them alongside the driveway.

"What about short boards?" Katie asked. "How does this work for them?"

"If they are a little short, we'll just tie them to the longer boards before we attach them to the bike. If they are a lot short, I can put them in my scout backpack." Darius took his empty orange backpack from where it was leaning against the garage and put it on his back. "And I have gloves, too."

"You've thought of everything."

"Let's hope so. I'll just tell my mom we're going for a bike ride. We've got to get moving if we're going to get there before the builders leave at five."

4

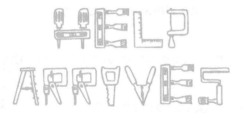

he ride to the construction site took them downhill for about a half mile, then back up and down a few times until the final uphill climb to where the new house stood on a ridge. They arrived to see the stack of wood scraps even higher than before.

Darius and Katie both waved, and the workers waved back.

This time, a woman in a hard hat, wearing an orange t-shirt, jeans, and a leather tool belt approached them. "Dennis tells me you're here for the wood."

"Yes, we are, if that's still okay," said Darius.

"Of course. There's plenty more. I'm Beverly, by the way. Dennis is the job foreman. I'm the project manager."

"I'm Darius, and this is my friend, Katie."

"I'm his assistant," Katie joked, "but I'd like to be a project manager, too."

Darius changed the subject. "That's going to be a big house."

"Yes, it is. Three thousand, five hundred square feet."

"Wow." Darius had no idea how big a normal size house was, but he sensed by the way Beverly said the number that it was enormous.

She continued, "Five bedrooms, four bathrooms, a finished basement with a home theater, and a second-floor balcony that lets you see Happy Lake in the distance. I'll give you guys a tour when we're closer to finishing."

"That would be awesome," Darius said.

She walked back up the long drive. He and Katie got to work sorting through the wood and arranging it by size. Katie tied a few pieces across her basket while Darius used his bungee cord contraption to attach longer boards to his bike.

While they were working, they didn't hear another bike approach until it skidded to a stop on the gravel.

"Hey, you two. Taking more wood, I see."

"Joe," exclaimed Katie, brushing her hands on her shorts. "Building up those leg muscles, again."

"Coach says I need endurance, not just strength." He reached down and retrieved a water bottle from its holder attached to the bike frame. "I have to do twelve miles now, then fifteen next week."

Darius lifted the full backpack onto his back. It

was then he realized he couldn't get on his bike with boards blocking the seat on both sides.

Joe leaned his bike against the fence and unhooked one side of the boards, letting Darius mount his bike.

"Thanks," said Darius as Joe reattached the boards.

When Darius started down the road, the weight of the backpack made it difficult to pedal and balance, and the bungeed boards made steering precarious.

"This is not going as planned," admitted Darius.

"Let me take the backpack," Joe offered. "I'll follow you."

"Thanks."

Darius loosened the straps and wriggled out of the backpack. Joe slid his arms through the straps and adjusted them until the pack rested comfortably on his shoulders.

The three pedaled the ups and downs, taking their time to avoid dropping their loads.

"This is it," announced Darius as he pulled into his driveway. Katie and Joe followed. They helped each other unload the boards onto the stack Darius had started earlier.

Darius's mother opened the porch door. "Darius, your father is grilling burgers out back. Would your friends like to stay for dinner?"

"I'd love to, Mrs. Knight," answered Katie. She ran up the steps. "I'll just wash my hands in your bathroom."

Joe didn't say anything.

"Joe?" asked Darius.

"My mother says I shouldn't go to someone's house to eat without bringing something for the meal."

"You brought some wood, though."

"I didn't realize you were beavers," Joe commented.

"Ha. Please stay. Think of dinner as a thank you."

"Well, my mom's working, so I'd be eating alone at home."

"So, there you go. My dad makes great burgers." Darius led the way into the house where they could wash up.

By the time they got back outdoors, the burgers were about done. Darius introduced Joe to his parents, and everyone filled their plates with potato salad, baked beans, and burgers with all the fixings.

While the parents sat with Paulie at the patio table, Darius, Katie, and Joe sat cross-legged on a blanket spread on the soft grass nearby. Darius could sense his parents' curiosity about Joe. It wasn't like them to not ask questions. This time, he was hoping they'd ask questions because he was also curious about Joe.

It didn't take long.

"It is nice of you to help Darius and Katie," Darius's mother said. "Do you live around here?"

"I live right in Rocky Point. We have an apartment."

"So, what brings you way out here?"

Darius answered for him. "Joe's coach wants him to build up his endurance, so he has to ride a bike up in the hills. That's how we met."

"And it's a good thing, too," added Katie. "We needed more hands with all that wood."

"Speaking of which," Darius's father asked, "what do you plan to do with all that wood?"

"Well, you know that big oak tree there on the ridge?" Darius pointed to the tree near the back of their property. "I was thinking of building a treehouse."

"A treehouse? Not too high up, I hope," said his mother.

Darius answered, "Not too high, just a few feet. We could get a good view of Happy Lake."

His father looked skeptical. "Draw up some plans, and I'll have a look before you start."

Darius knew that was his father's way of saying yes. "Thanks, Dad."

Paulie came over and sat on the blanket next to Darius, staring at Joe.

"Hi, I'm Joe? What's your name?"

"Paulie."

"Nice to meet you, Paulie." Joe held out his hand, and Paulie shook it.

"You have big hands," Paulie said.

"They are good for catching a football. And throwing too." Joe made the motion of throwing a pass. "Do you like football?"

"A little," Paulie answered. "I'm not very good."

"I'll bring over my football and show you some tips."

"Really? Cool."

Darius's mother spoke. "You are so good with him, Joe. Do you have any brothers and sisters?"

"No. But I always wanted a little brother."

"So, just you and your parents?"

"Um. Me and my mom, mostly. My dad is overseas working."

"What does he do?" asked Darius's father.

"He . . . I'm not sure exactly."

Darius could sense that Joe was uncomfortable answering questions. "Say, let's go check out the tree and get some treehouse ideas."

Darius and Katie jumped up and started for the oak tree.

"Me, too?" asked Joe.

"Of course. You're part of the team now," Darius said.

"Team Treehouse," Katie enthused.

Joe stood up. "I like it."

The three new friends wasted no time heading to the side yard with Paulie tagging along.

As they approached the tree, a dog came running through the bushes toward them, panting and wagging its tail, causing Joe to take a step back.

"Champ, what are you doing here?" Darius asked as Champ nuzzled up against his legs. Champ made the rounds, sniffing Katie, Joe, and Paulie, then he ran off toward the backyard with Paulie close behind.

"I don't think Champ's here for us," said Joe, "I think he smells the burgers."

"You are probably right," said Katie.

"How does it feel to be second place to a piece of meat?" Joe asked. "So much for being man's best friend."

Darius smirked. "You could wear a dress made out of meat like Lady Gaga did. I'm sure he'd be your best friend then."

"No thanks," Katie said. "I'll settle for being second place."

The three went back to examining the tree.

Pointing up, Darius said, "If we build it so the floor sits above that split, it will be sturdier, I think. We'll need—"

Mr. Wilson emerged from the undergrowth between their properties. "I'm very sorry. Champ got away again."

"Not a problem, Mr. Wilson," Darius assured him. "Champ is always welcome. And you, too, of course."

Mr. Wilson laughed. "Thanks, but I don't want to intrude." He looked up the tree. "But may I ask what you were looking at? A squirrel?"

"I was thinking of building a treehouse in this tree. We were just trying to come up with ideas on how to build it."

"I might be able to help with that. I still have a lot of carpentry tools in my barn."

"That would be great," Darius said. "The only thing I ever built before was a birdhouse."

"That was when we were in kindergarten," Katie reminded him. "I'm not sure that counts, seeing as our parents did most of the work."

"It's the only experience I have."

Everyone laughed, and Mr. Wilson waved his hand. "I don't want to interrupt your evening. Just let me know when you want to get together."

"Sounds great," answered Darius.

Mr. Wilson called Champ from his playtime with Paulie, and off they went back through the bushes.

Darius turned to Katie and Joe. "Once I get a big pile of wood here, I'll get him to help us."

"Don't forget the nails," Joe said, "that is—unless you plan on taping it all together."

Darius put a hand to his chin. "Hmmm. Duct tape, maybe."

"I can't tell if you two are being serious or are kidding around," Katie said.

The boys looked at each other, then laughed.

5

PLANS

66 got your text," said Joe as he swung his leg over his bike frame and coasted to a stop, "but I was in school until three. Did your school let out early today?"

"I don't go to school. My brother and I are home-schooled. So is Katie."

"I've heard of homeschooling, but I never met anybody who was home-schooled. How does it work?"

"We do our academic subjects, math, science, social studies, and language arts in the mornings. Then we have the afternoon to do activities, work on projects, or go on field trips with other home-schoolers. We get together with other home-schoolers to have art and music classes. For P.E., Katie takes dance classes and is on a soccer team. I just finished a juggling workshop. Some days, like today, we are free."

"How do you know what to learn? Like for math or science."

"We have a curriculum. Mostly online."

"A what?"

"A curriculum. It tells us what to study in an order that makes sense. I like homeschooling because if I get stuck, I can redo something at my own pace. It's mostly online, so if something is easy, I go faster. No waiting for anyone else. The best part is, if I get done early, I'm done. No sitting around waiting for school to end."

"I wish I could do that. Math is easy and class is sometimes boring, but I always feel like I need more time in English. The class moves on before I get it. I'm barely passing. If I fail the next test, I won't be able to play in the next baseball game."

"My mom is really good at English, especially writing. She used to work for a newspaper. Maybe she could help you."

"She'd think I was an idiot."

"She wouldn't. She helps me all the time when I get stuck on something. I'll ask her."

Before Joe could protest anymore, Darius ran into the house.

Moments later, Darius and his mother came outside.

"I'd be happy to help you. When is your test?"

"Next Tuesday."

"We have a few days. Bring over your work and we'll see what we can do."

"Thank you, Mrs. Knight. I hope you are not wasting your time."

"Time spent learning is never wasted. Tomorrow then? After dinner? If your mom is working, come for dinner, too."

"Thank you."

Mrs. Knight turned and went back inside.

"Your mom's so nice to do this. I would have said no, but I really need to pass this test," Joe said. It almost sounded like an apology.

"I want you to pass the test. Think positive. You will pass the test."

"You sound like my mother."

"Good. I'm glad we think alike."

"I didn't come over to listen to my mother, though. What did you want?"

"Let me show you my plans for a treehouse." Darius ran back into the house and returned with a notebook and pencil. He opened to the first page and held it up for Joe to see. "I had to spend a lot of time Googling treehouse plans to get an idea of what we could do."

Joe looked over the plans but didn't say anything right away. Darius tried to figure out what Joe was thinking by watching his facial expressions, but he couldn't tell.

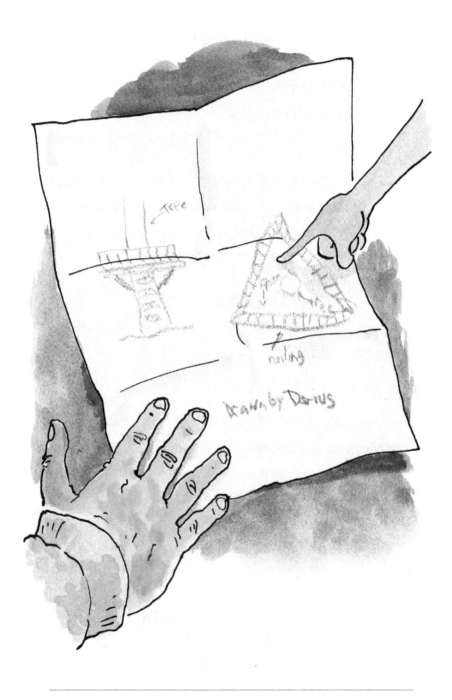

"Well?" Darius asked when he couldn't stand the suspense.

"I like it," Joe nodded, "but do we have the wood that we need to build it?"

"I took an inventory of all the pieces we already have and their sizes." Darius flipped to a different page in the notebook to show his list. "We almost have what we need. One more trip to the new house and we will have enough."

"And your dad says it's good?"

"Not yet. He's at work."

"Where does he work?"

"He's the CFO at Preston Enterprises. He handles the money end of the company."

"Preston? They're the ones that make machine parts?" Joe asked.

"Yeah, and a ton of other stuff."

"My mom worked there a few years ago for a while, but she got a job for an office cleaning company that paid better. No offense to your dad."

"None taken." Darius shrugged. "My dad is always telling me to get an education so I can have a career and not be stuck at a low-paying job. No offense to your mom."

"My mom was going to go to college, but after I was born, she didn't. But she wants me to go. She says

I need to get a sports scholarship to pay for college because she can't afford it. She doesn't want me to end up in low-paying jobs either. That's why I work so hard at sports, especially football."

"No chance of a sports scholarship for me. I have to do well in my academics. After Paulie was born, my mom decided to stay home with us and homeschool me so I could work at my own pace. My mom works part-time as an editor for a publishing company. But enough about that. I want to find out what Mr. Wilson thinks of my treehouse plan."

"He was sitting on his porch when I rode by," Joe said.

"Great. We should go over there now." Darius grabbed his bike and hopped on.

"Why don't we go through the back way?" asked Joe.

"I don't like sneaking up on him. I wouldn't want to scare him, especially when he's offered to help."

"Good point."

It only took a minute to ride to Mr. Wilson's where he sat with Champ on the old farmhouse's large front porch.

"Greetings, boys."

"Hi, Mr. Wilson," Darius began, "I drew up some plans for a treehouse. Would you look them over and tell me what you think?"

"Of course."

The two boys stepped onto the porch and gave Champ some pats and chin scratches.

Mr. Wilson looked over the sketch carefully. "Your railings should be a little higher for safety reasons. And there needs to be some more bracing. I would use triangles. They are much sturdier than a square. Before you begin, you'll want to have exact measurements for every board." He leaned over to a little table and picked up a pencil from on top of the newspaper's crossword page. He jotted down a few numbers and added a few lines to the sketch while Darius and Joe watched.

"You're good at this," Darius said.

"I've done a little woodworking in my day," replied Mr. Wilson. "Now, I recommend you use screws to put this together. Much sturdier, and if you ever want to make changes, it's easier to take apart."

"That's going to take a lot of time," Darius said.

"Not to mention sore wrists," added Joe.

"Not with the right tools. Follow me."

Mr. Wilson led them around the house to his backyard and over to his large barn far back on his property. It looked like it had been built many years ago when the land around here was all farms. The wood siding was weathered grey. He opened the door and switched on the overhead lights.

"Wow," was all Darius could say.

The interior of the barn was a large modern woodworking workshop. Stationed around the room were two table saws, a lathe, and a drill press. On shelves along the wall were smaller tools, circular saws, drills, jigsaws, and many Darius couldn't even guess. A few pieces of partially completed furniture were lined against the back wall. From the colors, Darius could tell that there were many different types of wood being used.

Joe spoke up. "This is quite impressive, Mr. Wilson."

"Thank you. Even though I'm retired, I still like to putter." Mr. Wilson walked over to one of the tool shelves. "Here's what we need." He lifted the battery-powered drill and handed it to Darius. "I'll show you how to use that. It makes quick work of putting boards together. Always remember, having the right tools for the right job makes things much easier."

Darius wasn't sure how all of this would work, but he had a huge smile on his face. "This is great, Mr. Wilson. I just hope my dad okays the plans."

6

NEW SKILLS

fter a discussion with Mr. Wilson, Darius's father gave his approval of the plans. Katie and Darius got to work measuring the boards and laying them out. When Mr. Wilson found out the kids were going to use a handsaw to cut the wood, he offered to bring over his sawhorses, clamps, and power saw to speed things along.

"I wonder where Joe is this morning," said Katie. "He said he'd help with the heavy stuff."

"I think he has a game today. It's almost the end of the season and he said his team is doing really well." Darius also wished Joe would be there soon. "I hope they win."

"Should we text him?"

"I don't want to bother him if he's in the middle of a game. I'm sure he'll come over when he can."

Mr. Wilson pulled into the Knight's driveway in his old pickup truck. Darius and Katie ran over to help him unload his tools.

"Hey," exclaimed Darius, "You picked up those pieces of plywood."

"Yes, I explained to the foreman that I was picking them up for you, and he just waved and kept working."

"We have our floor now," said Katie.

Mr. Wilson showed them how to set up the sawhorses and clamp a board.

Katie pointed out that even the sawhorses were triangles, so they were stronger. "Now we can start cutting."

"We're not quite ready to saw yet," said Mr. Wilson. He reached into his tool bag and pulled out three pairs of safety glasses. "Safety first."

He took the time to explain how the circular saw worked, how to line it up, and how to move it slowly along the wood. Then he demonstrated by cutting the first piece.

"Only five hundred more to go," he joked. "Why don't you give it a try." He motioned to Darius. "Your dad said it would be okay as long as I supervised."

"I'll admit, I'm a little nervous."

"Understandably," Mr. Wilson said. "It's a new skill. Take your time."

They positioned a new board on the sawhorses and clamped it down. Darius held on to the saw, pressing the safety button and trigger. The saw whirred to life. Darius moved the saw across the board and completed the cut.

"Pretty easy, huh?" asked Mr. Wilson. "You'll be a pro in no time." He turned to Katie. "Would you like to try?"

"Sure, I can't let Darius have all the fun."

Katie's cut went as smooth as the others'. "This is so cool."

***

The morning passed quickly while they worked. By noon, most of the boards had been measured, checked twice, and cut. As they finished each piece, they assembled the platform as it would look when put up in the tree.

Mr. Wilson took off his safety glasses and unplugged the saw from its extension cord. "Time to take Champ home for his lunch. I'll be back over with my ladder this afternoon. Between my ladder and your dad's, we should be able to start mounting boards on the tree."

"Super. My mom will be home this afternoon to help Paulie with his school project, so my dad will be able to help also," said Darius. "And I think Joe will be here, too."

"Many hands make light work," said Mr. Wilson. "An old expression, but it's true." He whistled and Champ came running, hopping into the pickup truck's cab as soon as the door opened.

Darius and Katie went inside to wash up for lunch.

"It doesn't look like much yet, but I'm excited to see it go up," Darius said, as they sat at the table with his father and Paulie.

"Mr. Wilson said your plans were solid," his father said. "An architect in the making were his words."

"Really?" Darius blushed.

"I picked up the screws at the hardware store he suggested."

"And duct tape?" Katie asked.

Darius's father looked puzzled.

"Just a little joke, Mr. Knight," Katie said laughing.

"You had me worried there for a minute. I thought I forgot to get something."

***

After lunch, Darius helped his father carry their ladder from the garage and lean it against the tree. They brought out a smaller step ladder just in case.

Mr. Wilson pulled in and climbed down from his truck.

"No Champ?"

"He's having a siesta. He'll find us, don't worry."

Darius and Katie brought the ladder from the back of his pickup and leaned it against the opposite side of the tree.

"I wonder how old this tree is," remarked Katie.

Mr. Wilson looked up. "I've lived next door all my

life, and it was a big old tree when I was a boy. I'd guess it's a hundred and fifty years old or more."

"Wow," said Katie.

"It's oak, so it's sturdy," Mr. Wilson continued. "They can live for hundreds of years."

Even though Darius found the information interesting, he was eager to get started putting the treehouse together.

"Floor frame first?" he asked.

"Sure thing," Mr. Wilson said, grabbing one end of a frame board while Darius picked up the other end and headed for the tree.

"Not so fast. To the sawhorses, young man, "Mr. Wilson directed.

Darius was confused but put on his safety glasses as directed.

"I'll teach you a secret to working with screws. Drill pilot holes first. That way, the screw knows where to go when you put it in. No crooked messes. And sometimes, you can even start the screw in the board, so you only have to finish it once it's in place. In fact, we might want to do that here because we'll be up in the air. Hard to hold a ladder, a board, a drill, and a screw all at once."

"I'm learning so much, Mr. Wilson," Darius gushed.

"Like I said, you'll be a pro in no time."

Climbing up a ladder while holding on to a heavy board was much harder than Darius anticipated, but he was determined to do this.

Mr. Wilson guided the board and fastened it into place above the split trunk.

Katie and Darius took turns on the stepladder to hold up the boards as they positioned them. Mr. Wilson would screw in his end, while the kids took turns on the other.

After about an hour, most of the floor frame was secured.

"Time for a break?" asked Darius's father stepping outside with a tray of lemonade and cookies.

"Thanks, Dad." Darius and the others stopped working and walked over to the picnic table in the backyard.

"You guys are doing a great job. And thank you, Mr. Wilson. About all I know how to build is a birdhouse. I'm afraid I have to hire all of my carpentry work done."

"Not for long." Mr. Wilson patted Darius on the back.

"A birdhouse?" Katie asked, with a crooked grin. "I remember that birdhouse." She and Darius laughed, leaving the adults with confused looks on their faces.

They finished their snacks and headed back to the tree.

Darius noticed that Mr. Wilson was looking tired. "Mr. Wilson, do you mind if we just do a little more and then stop for the day? I want my friend Joe to be here to learn some of this, too."

"Sure thing. I was just thinking I might need to check on Champ."

Darius, his father, Katie, and Mr. Wilson positioned three triangular braces under the floor.

"That ought to hold her until tomorrow," said Mr. Wilson. He reached out to shake Darius's and Katie's hands. "To my best students."

"You're a great teacher," said Katie.

"I agree," added Darius.

Once Mr. Wilson had pulled out of the driveway, Darius took out his phone.

"There's a message from Joe." He read it to himself. "Oh, no!"

"What?" Katie asked. "What?"

"Joe's in the hospital. He got injured in the game."

7

arius read the rest of the message out loud. "A possible concussion and a dislocated knee. He's got to stay overnight for observation."

"That sounds bad," Katie said. "We should go visit him."

Darius turned to his father, "Dad, can you take us to the hospital?"

"Of course. I think it would cheer him up. I'll let your mother know we're going." He bounded up the steps and into the house.

Katie called her mother, but Darius could tell it was not going well when Katie walked around the corner of the house to finish the conversation in private.

Returning, Katie said, "I can't go. We've got company coming for dinner and I have to get home to help get ready. I totally forgot. Please tell Joe I hope he gets better soon."

"I will."

Katie was already on her bike when Darius's father walked out onto the porch. "Your mother is sending us with cookies."

As he saw Katie leaving, Darius informed him of her situation.

"That's too bad. Katie always has cheerful things to say."

Darius and his father climbed into the family's grey SUV and Darius took charge of the bag of cookies. Being alone with his father in the vehicle meant he got to sit in the front seat. Every time, he imagined what it would be like to drive.

***

The hospital wasn't as scary this time. The last time Darius was here, Paulie was at the emergency room with a rash and fever in the middle of the night.

Darius's father signed them in, then directed them to the elevators.

"Room 304," said the receptionist, looking over her reading glasses.

They arrived at room 304 and knocked at the open door. The curtain surrounding one of the beds swung back and a tall woman with straight, shoulder-length brown hair looked at them. Darius noticed she was wearing jeans and a flower print blouse, not at all dressed like any of the nurses.

"Yes?" she asked.

"We're here to see Joe," said Darius.

From behind the curtain came Joe's voice. "Darius, come in."

"My dad's here, too."

"He can come in." As they entered Joe continued, "Hi, Mr. Knight. Mom, this is my friend Darius and his dad."

"Nice to meet you, I'm Debra. Debra Newman. Joe's mother. It's nice of you to visit. Joe's never been to a hospital before. It's . . ."

"A little scary?" offered Darius looking at the wires running from Joe's chest to machines and an IV attached to a pole beside his bed.

"More like embarrassing," said Joe. "Like my nightgown?"

"Cute," Darius answered. "Oh, here, my mom sent you some cookies." He handed the bag to Joe. "But if you're not allowed to eat them here, I'll take them back."

"Not a chance." Joe held the bag away from Darius, then peeked inside. "Nice."

Joe's mother placed a hand on Joe's arm. "Honey, I need to get to work. Will you be alright?"

"Yes, Mom. I'll be fine." He held up the bag. "I have cookies."

She kissed him on the cheek and said her good-byes to Darius and his father.

As she left, an older nurse in pale blue scrubs came to the door. "Ten minutes. He needs to rest."

"Noted," said Darius's father. "Thank you."

With that, the nurse turned and left.

"What happened?" Darius asked.

"Well, I was sliding into home and a player for the other team stepped in front of me and my leg got twisted. That's the knee part. When I rolled over, the baseball being thrown home hit me in the head."

"Ouch."

"Coach yelled 'Don't move,' so I laid on the baseline. People must have thought I was dead, for sure. I couldn't tell what hurt worse, my head or my knee. Before I knew it, they put me on a stretcher and into an ambulance with ice packs all over."

"All over the ambulance?"

It took Joe a little while to get the joke, but Darius was glad to see he still had his sense of humor.

"Yes, I thought I was in an ice cream truck with a really bad tune playing."

Darius was now caught in his own slow understanding. "The siren. I get it," he said finally.

"I hope we're not driving you nuts, Mr. Knight," Joe said.

"Not at all. Nice to see you are in good spirits. Did the doctors give you any information?"

"Well, the ER doctor said my knee didn't really dislocate, it's just strained and should be fine in a week or so. They want me to stay here hooked up to all this stuff tonight to make sure I don't have a serious concussion. I was never unconscious, so that's a good sign," he said.

"You're right about that," said Darius's father.

While they were talking, Darius looked at the name tag on Joe's wrist.

"That says your name is Jose."

Joe covered the tag with his other hand. "Yeah, but I go by Joe. Jose is my father's name."

"Does your dad know you are in the hospital?" asked Darius's father.

Joe didn't respond, he just looked toward the window.

"I'm sorry. I didn't mean to upset you."

Joe's eyes swelled. "I need to tell you something. I kind of didn't tell you the whole truth the other day. My dad works overseas, but that's not it, really. After my parents got married and my mother was expecting me, he decided to go back to Brazil and not come back. His name was Jose, so my mom named me after him when I was born hoping he'd change his mind. But she gave me her maiden name, Newman, so I would feel a part of her family, too."

"Your mom sounds like a smart lady," Darius's father said.

"She is," replied Joe, wiping away a tear. "I just hope I can still play football this fall without any more injuries, or I can kiss any sports scholarships goodbye."

"It's too soon to worry about that. Just follow the doctor's orders and get yourself well."

Joe nodded, but he put his hand to his forehead. "Still hurts to move my head quickly."

"Hey, I almost forgot," Darius said. He pulled out his phone and showed a picture of the treehouse in progress.

"That's looking good." Joe took the phone and studied the photo.

"Mr. Wilson has been teaching us a lot about building. Even if you can't help yet, you should come over and learn some stuff."

"As soon as I can."

Movement at the door caught their attention. The same nurse stood there smiling and tapping her wrist.

"Just about to go," said Darius's father. "Well, boys, that's it."

Joe handed the phone back to Darius.

"Let me know when you get home," Darius said.

"Yup," Joe said with a small wave.

The nurse ushered them out.

***

Once back in the SUV, Darius asked, "Do you think Joe will be able to play football well enough to get a scholarship?"

"I don't see why not. He's a growing boy. He'll heal fast. I broke my leg skiing when I was in school. I'm fine now."

"You never told me that."

"It never came up before. I was out the rest of the season, but the next year, I was back on the slopes. Good as new. And a good thing, too. That's where I met your mother. On the ski slopes in college."

"I knew you met in college, but not skiing."

"Do what you like, and you'll meet people you like. That's usually how it goes."

Darius thought about that for a few minutes as they drove home.

As they turned the corner onto their road, Darius noticed a black sedan pulled over in front of their house. Darius's father turned into the driveway and parked.

They could see a tall thin man in a baggy white shirt and baggy tan pants held up by a narrow black belt standing in their side yard looking up toward the half-finished treehouse. His hands were on his hips, and Darius could see the top of his bald head above the ring of short grey hair.

"May I help you?" Darius's father asked as they walked over to the man.

"I stopped by to see what was going on here."

"The kids are building a treehouse."

"I'm Cyril Bridgewater, town building inspector and code enforcement officer." He handed Darius's father a business card. "There is no permit on file to build this. I'm afraid it will have to come down."

"What?" shouted Darius.

8

TROUBLE FOR THE TREEHOUSE

"He can't do that, can he?" Darius asked after Bridgewater pulled onto the road.

"Apparently so," his father replied.

"But do I have to take it down?"

"That's what he said."

"Can't we just get a permit to finish it?"

"That is a very good question, Darius. A very good question. Why don't we get Mr. Wilson's opinion on the matter before we do anything. He's lived here his whole life, and I think he worked for the town at one point."

Darius was able to calm down when he heard that.

"Let's get some dinner," said Darius's father.

After dinner, Darius got another text from Katie.

Darius dialed. "Hey, you won't believe what just happened?"

"What? Is Joe okay?"

Darius wasn't even thinking about Joe just then. "Yeah, he's just in the hospital for observation. The doctors said he'll be fine. He's got cookies."

There was a pause, then Katie spoke. "I'm confused. You said I wouldn't believe what happened. What happened?"

Darius told her all about the arrival of the building inspector.

"Take it down?" she shouted into the phone. "What kind of meanie doesn't let kids have a treehouse?"

"The building inspector kind, I guess. Can you come over tomorrow after lunch? We're going to talk to Mr. Wilson about it."

"Sure."

***

Darius and Katie watched from the living room window as an older model green car pulled into the driveway. They ran out.

"Joe! You're here," shouted Katie. As Joe lifted himself out of the passenger side, she added, "Nice brace."

"Thanks. I have to wear it for a few days if I go out. Just in case. And I have to take it easy for my head." He pulled a pair of crutches from the back seat and used them to cross the lawn toward the oak tree.

His mother followed but stopped when she saw Darius's father. "Thank you so much, Mr. Knight, for allowing him to come over while I work. I worry with him home by himself."

"Mom, I'm fourteen," Joe said, but his voice cracked a little. He turned and continued to the backyard where Katie had set up two lawn chairs, one for him to sit in and one to put his leg on.

Mr. Wilson arrived a short time later and sat at the picnic table across from Darius as he recounted the incident with the building inspector. Katie and Darius's father listened from their places at the table.

"Bilgewater, you say?" Mr. Wilson scratched his chin.

"Bridgewater," Darius corrected him.

"Yes, I heard you. Bilgewater and I go way back."

Darius looked up at his father who was trying not to laugh.

"What?" Darius asked. "What's so funny?"

Mr. Wilson explained. "Cyril Bridgewater and I both grew up here. He always wanted to be telling people what to do, even in elementary school. The building inspector job lets him do just that. Way back in high school, a substitute teacher misread his name during attendance as Bilgewater instead of Bridgewater. Ever since then, it's been a nickname people use when he gets too high and mighty acting. I suppose it's not very nice."

"What is bilgewater?" asked Katie.

"It's the nasty, mucky water that is in the very bottom of a ship," Mr. Wilson explained.

Darius wouldn't say it out loud, but he was thinking, Bilgewater suits Cyril Bridgewater perfectly.

"Now, let's get to work." Mr. Wilson said.

"But–" Darius began.

"I'll handle Mr. Bilgewater. Don't worry." Mr. Wilson smiled.

With that, Katie and Darius helped Joe sit near the tree so he would be closer to the action. Then they set about adding more bracing and placed the plywood on the frame for the floor.

"Now, we get to build the ladder up the tree trunk," said Darius.

"I think it's time for a coffee break. Don't you, Mr. Wilson?" Darius's dad asked.

"I could use one."

"I'll bring you a cup out to the picnic table." He walked up the steps into the house while Mr. Wilson headed over to the table.

"We'll just keep working if that's okay, Mr. Wilson," Darius said.

"Sure thing."

"And I'll just keep supervising," joked Joe.

Darius drilled a pilot hole in the center of the

board, then screwed a long screw into the tree so the board was tight against the trunk.

He repeated this with four more boards and placed them about a foot apart up the tree.

"Now give it a try," called Mr. Wilson.

Darius held on to the top step and put his foot on the bottom. As he put his weight on the step, the board gave way beneath him, swinging to a vertical position along the trunk. His foot was back on the ground.

Mr. Wilson laughed.

"Hey, you knew that was going to happen," Darius said, getting red in the face.

"I had a feeling," Mr. Wilson replied.

"Why didn't you say something?"

Mr. Wilson walked back over to the tree. "If I had just told you, you might not remember. But finding out for yourself is a lesson learned."

Darius turned the step back into its horizontal position.

"Now the question is how do we keep it from spinning?" Mr. Wilson looked at the kids with his eyebrows raised.

"Put a brace on each step?" offered Joe.

"Might work," Mr. Wilson answered.

"Use more than one screw so it can't spin?" asked Darius.

"Let's try that first. If that doesn't work, we'll try braces."

They set about drilling pilot holes and adding screws to each step.

"Now for the test," Darius announced. He held on and took a step up. "So far, so good." He took two more steps until there were no more places to hang on.

"You did it, young man," Mr. Wilson said, clapping.

"We need to add some more steps for handholds, though, so we can climb high enough to step onto the floor."

"Then I want to have a turn," Katie said.

"Well, well," said Mr. Wilson looking toward the road. The rest of the group turned to see what he was looking at and watched a black sedan inch along the road as it approached their house, then drive away.

Darius asked, "Wasn't that—"

"Bilgewater," Mr. Wilson interrupted, answering the question. "Now he knows we didn't take down the treehouse."

"What will he do now?" asked Katie.

The kids looked at Mr. Wilson.

"He doesn't like to be ignored, so I imagine you'll hear from him soon."

The sound of a car approaching from the opposite

direction got their attention. Bridgewater was making another slow pass.

"Soon is right," Joe said, but Bridgewater didn't stop. "I've never met him, but I'm beginning to not like that guy."

"You said it, young man," Mr. Wilson said, clapping.

9

SPECIAL DELIVERY

When Darius rolled out of bed Monday morning, he headed straight to the bedroom window. He sighed. It looked like it was going to be an all-day rain.

Darius finished his morning schoolwork shortly after Paulie finished his, so they played video games until lunch. Darius used to feel bad when Paulie lost almost every game, but lately, he felt bad about himself losing almost every game.

Darius looked out the kitchen window toward the oak tree and half-finished treehouse. *Without a roof, it's just a wet deck,* he thought. He checked online for tomorrow's weather. *Sunny and seventy-eight. Awesome!*

Paulie interrupted his thoughts. "Will Joe be able to walk again?"

"Sure, in no time."

"Good, because he's going to teach me football."

"Just don't pester him about it," Darius advised.

"I won't. He offered."

Their mother walked into the kitchen just then. "Are you talking about Joe? I'm going to do a zoom

call with him at one since he's home from school today. Tomorrow is his writing test, so this is our last opportunity."

"Can you ask him when he can teach me football?"

"No pestering," Darius reminded him.

"I think today we should just let Joe focus on preparing for his test."

***

Tuesday, as predicted, was sunny and warm.

Katie was the first to arrive mid-afternoon. "I would have been here sooner, but my dance class ran over," she said as she hopped off her bike and leaned it against the lamppost by the front walk.

"That's okay. Mr. Wilson said he'd come over at three thirty." Darius said. "And Joe said he'd be here, too."

Behind her, a grey car driven by an older man was pulling into the driveway. In the passenger seat, they could see an older woman waving.

"Do you know them?" Katie asked.

"Never saw them before in my life," Darius replied. He stepped down off the porch and stood next to Katie.

The back door of the car opened.

"Hey, you guys. It's me." Joe stuck his head out

the door. "Meet my grandparents. They came down from Cleveland to help out so my mom doesn't have to miss work, even though I told her I can take care of myself."

Darius and Katie greeted Joe's grandparents as Joe got out of the car.

"No crutches?"

"The doctor said I could stop using them as soon as I felt good enough, but I still have to wear the brace until I see him again. Oh, Darius, is it okay to show my grandpa the treehouse? I told him about it."

"Sure."

Joe waved for his grandfather to come. When he stood after exiting the car, Darius said aloud, "Wow, Joe. I see how you got to be so big and tall."

"That's what my mom says. If I'm lucky, I'll get to be six three like my grandpa. Right, Grandpa?"

"And spend your life ducking through doorways like I have. Lucky? Sure," he said, laughing.

The three kids led him behind the house to the tree.

"I must say, that looks mighty sturdy," Joe's grandfather said as he walked around the tree. "Good bracing."

"We had help," Darius explained, "Our neighbor, Mr. Wilson, knows a lot about carpentry. He's teach-

ing us things like the strength of triangles and what tools to use."

"Knowing how to build things is a great skill to have." He put his arm around Joe and gave his shoulders a squeeze. "School isn't the only place to learn." Joe nodded.

"Speaking of school, Joe, how did your test go?" asked Darius.

"I thought it went okay, so I saw the teacher after school. She said I passed with a B-plus. I need to thank your mom."

"My smart grandson." Joe's grandfather turned to Darius and Katie. "It was nice to meet you both. Joe, what time should we pick you up?"

Joe looked at Darius.

"Eight would be fine," Darius answered for him. "He's welcome for dinner, so we can work on the treehouse while the weather is good."

"Oh, I almost forgot. I have something in the car," Joe said.

The group walked back to the car where Joe's grandmother was waiting with her window down.

Joe leaned in and gave her a quick kiss on the cheek. "See you later." He opened the back door and pulled out a store-bought apple strudel. He handed it to Darius, "Mom sent this."

Darius's eyes lit up.

***

The kids knew Mr. Wilson was on his way through the wooded area between their houses when Champ raced into the yard.

"How is it that an old dog is faster than an old man?" Mr. Wilson asked as he pushed his way through the undergrowth. "Hello, fellow carpenters," he said noticing the kids by the treehouse. "I see you got the tools out already. An eager bunch, aren't you?"

"We want to get as much done as we can," Darius said.

"Of course. Well, first, we have a problem to solve. In order to put on a roof, we need to get those long supports on the corners of the floor." He pointed to the drawing in Darius's notebook. "I didn't see any boards long enough in your stash."

"I thought we could screw short ones together to make ones tall enough," Darius explained.

Mr. Wilson scratched his chin. "I'm thinking about safety. They will have to support the whole weight of the roof."

Katie asked, "We probably should just buy the right boards then, huh?"

Darius could feel himself getting frustrated. *So, we can't do anything today,* he thought. Just great. He

straightened his shoulders and asked, "What can we do without them?"

"How about we go over to my barn for a few minutes? I think I may have a solution."

The kids looked at each other and followed Mr. Wilson back through the bushes.

Instead of going into the barn, he led them behind it where an overhanging roof covered a stack of weathered wood.

"I think we can find what we need here." Mr. Wilson winked at them and smiled.

They moved a few boards until Mr. Wilson spotted what he was looking for. "These four-by-fours will be perfect. I hope you are ready to lug these back to your house, Darius."

"With help, I hope."

Everyone laughed. Between them, they carried the boards to the work area.

"I just realized something," said Joe. "These four-by-fours are very heavy to get up to the treehouse floor. Especially if we have to walk up a ladder and try to keep them balanced."

"We could use two ladders and have two people carry a board up to lay on the floor," suggested Katie.

"Or we could hook up a pulley on the branch above the floor," suggested Darius.

"Pulleys make it easier to lift heavy objects."

"Yes, that's true," said Mr. Wilson, "if you have a block and tackle."

"A what?" asked Joe. "Tackle, like in fishing?"

"Not exactly," Mr. Wilson said, chuckling.

"I thought of another problem," said Joe. "If we stand those four-by-fours up on the corners, how do we attach them so they don't fall over."

"Temporary braces," answered Katie. "I learned that from the construction site."

"Cool."

Mr. Wilson held up his hand. "All good ideas. But might I suggest we do something first?"

Darius asked, "Like what?"

"Why don't we build the railings and cut the roof pieces while everything is on the ground? Then move everything into place when we're ready."

"Mr. Wilson, great idea," said Darius. "That will give me time to work out a pulley system, too."

"So, everyone agrees?" asked Mr. Wilson.

"Yes," the kids answered in unison. They got busy measuring, cutting, and putting together the railings.

Everything was going smoothly until they started on the roof.

"Your drawing doesn't say exactly what the slant angle is on the roof, so we don't know how long to make the boards," said Joe.

"I wasn't sure about that. I figured we could just measure as we built it."

"There is a mathematical way to figure out how long the boards should be," said Mr. Wilson.

"Math, my specialty," exclaimed Joe.

"You can use the Pythagorean Theorem."

"The what?" Darius asked.

"Hey, I just learned that in school," Joe said. "A squared plus B squared equals C squared."

"Correct." Mr. Wilson pointed to Darius's drawing as he explained. If you know how long the bottom of the roof is, and you know the height so that you get a good pitch, you can figure out how long the diagonal board should be."

They measured the floor and height. Joe pulled out his phone and used the calculator to get an answer. "There you go." Joe held up his phone for all to see.

"I've got to learn that," Darius said.

"Me, too," added Katie.

"Your mom helps me, I help you." Joe grinned.

"Let's help ourselves to some dinner," Darius said. "You're invited, too, Mr. Wilson."

Darius was the last in. He watched his friends and felt happy, partly because they were having fun together and partly because they were making a place to call their own. *If only that Bilgewater guy doesn't get his way.*

Darius tried to put the thought out of his mind.

10

WORKING TOGETHER

he next few days were overcast and drizzly. For the most part, Darius and Paulie continued their usual rainy-day routine, schoolwork, video games, and TV. Only this time, Darius studied up on using a block and tackle. Buying one was out of the question. It would use up the money he had been saving for headphones.

One evening, he asked his father if they had any pulleys to make a block and tackle.

"No, but we could probably make something that would work." They headed out to the garage and looked through cabinets for suitable parts. A couple of long bolts, dowels with holes drilled through the center, and small frames to hold everything together took them about an hour.

"What about rope?" asked Darius.

Darius's father pulled a box off the top of the cabinet. "I bought this rope last year intending to put up a tire swing from the oak tree, but I never got to it. You might as well use it for the block and tackle."

"Thanks. Now to wait for good weather."

***

On the first sunny warm day, Darius was eager to try out his homemade block and tackle, but he had a field trip with his homeschool group. Since it was in Happy Lake, Darius and Katie decided to ride their bikes and meet the group at the library where a portable planetarium had been set up in the community room.

"I love this stuff," whispered Katie as they sat in the planetarium's dome watching the lights dim and the stars appear. For the rest of the hour, they sat listening to the instructor describe the constellations visible in each season, how the planets seem to move forward and back from our point of view, and how sailors used to navigate by the positions of certain stars.

When it was over and they crawled out of the planetarium's exit tunnel, everyone was squinting at the brightness.

"I almost forgot it was daytime," Darius said.

They had permission to stay at the library. Katie needed to pick up another book off her reading list. Darius signed out his first two. "I'd better get started."

On the way home, they took the shorter route. The treehouse was waiting to be finished.

As they passed a small cottage, an elderly woman waved from her porch.

Ethan A. Wohlwend

"Hi, Mrs. Baker," Katie called. She whispered to Darius, "I know her from church."

When the old woman answered, Katie turned and pulled into her driveway. Darius followed. They rode up to the porch and hopped off their bikes.

As Katie and Mrs. Baker talked, Darius noticed that one of the boards on the side of her steps was quite rotted. The steps were sloped down on that side. He could imagine how dangerous that could be, especially in the winter. He tapped Katie's arm and pointed to the steps.

"Your steps look like they need some help, Mrs. Baker."

"I suppose they do, but I just walk on the good side and hold the railing."

That didn't sound too safe to Darius, so he began to plan. He said nothing to Mrs. Baker about it because he had to make sure his plan was possible.

"It was nice to see you, Mrs. Baker," Katie said. "We need to get going."

"Be safe," she replied.

Once Darius and Katie got back on the road, Darius said, "I'm more worried about her being safe than us. Her steps are dangerous."

"I know."

"What do you say we fix them for her? We can use

one of the two-by-twelves to cut a new side piece and screw the steps into it."

"That would be great."

"I need to borrow Mr. Wilson's drill. I think he'll let me. Let's stop and ask."

Mr. Wilson was agreeable and lent the drill. Katie put it into her bike basket next to their books.

"Next stop, my house for a board, a measuring tape, some screws, and a saw."

They retrieved the items and told Darius's mother what they were doing for Mrs. Baker.

"She will be thrilled," Darius's mother said.

Once Darius attached the saw to the two-by-twelve and secured it using his bungee method, they hustled back to Mrs. Baker's cottage. She was still sitting on her porch when they arrived.

"Step repair service, Mrs. Baker," Katie announced.

"Oh, my!"

They got to work measuring and cutting the two-by-twelve to the right length with the correct angles.

"Uh oh," said Darius, examining the rotting board. "I think we need a hammer."

Mrs. Baker said," I have one. I think in my husband's toolbox." She went inside.

"Why doesn't her husband fix the stairs?" asked Darius.

"He died many years ago."

"Oh, that explains it then. Sorry."

Once Mrs. Baker returned with the hammer, Katie knocked the rotted board out of the way. Darius pulled the nails still attached to the loose step ends.

"Now I see why Mr. Wilson prefers screws to nails," he said putting all of his weight into his task.

Setting the new board in place and attaching the steps was easy. A few minutes later, the job was complete.

They hadn't noticed that Mrs. Baker went into the house. She returned with a tray of cookies and lemonade.

"For you hard workers," she said smiling. "But before you enjoy the treats," she pulled two five-dollar bills from her apron pocket and handed one to each of them.

"That's not necessary, Mrs. Baker," Darius protested.

"Nonsense, you provided me with a valuable service. It's the least I can do. Value for value, as it should be."

Darius couldn't argue with her logic. "Thank you," he said, tucking the money in his pocket. "Now do you want to try the stairs?"

"Why not?" She held onto the railing and stepped

tentatively down one step. "Oh, this is so nice. It's not springy anymore." A big smile stayed on her face for the last two steps. "Lovely."

"Glad you like it," Katie said.

The three sat on the porch enjoying the treats, Darius and Katie answering questions and listening to Mrs. Baker's stories.

"We need to get going now," said Katie when the conversation paused. "We have things to do at home."

"Of course. Don't let an old lady keep you," Mrs. Baker said, laughing. "Be safe."

***

It was after three when they arrived at Darius's house. Mr. Wilson was already at the treehouse, chatting with Paulie and their mother. Joe was by the sawhorses measuring some boards.

"Well, how did it go with Mrs. Baker's steps?" asked Mr. Wilson.

"Great," answered Darius. "She's thrilled like you said, Mom. And she insisted on paying us."

"Don't forget the lemonade and cookies," Katie added.

"I wish I were there," said Joe.

"For the food or the money?" Darius asked.

"Both."

Darius's mother jumped when the phone in her pocket started ringing. "Hello? . . . This is she. . . Why, thank you so much." She held up her hand while she listened. "We'll be expecting her call. Thank you again. Bye." She turned to Darius and his friends. "Well, that was Mrs. Baker."

"Uh oh," said Darius.

"No, it's a good thing. She was so happy to have her steps fixed that she called her friend who needs her steps fixed. Apparently, her friend doesn't use her back door anymore because of the bad steps. Anyway, Mrs. Baker called Katie's mom to get our number so she could call and see if it was alright to give her friend our number to find out if you kids wanted a job fixing her steps. Boy, that's a mouthful. Did everyone understand that?"

They nodded.

"It looks like you may have yourself a business opportunity," said Mr. Wilson. "Those old ladies have quite the hotline."

Joe started giggling. "You have taken the first steps to a new career."

Everyone groaned.

"That sounds like a joke my dad would tell," said Darius.

"One step at a time," Joe continued.

"Stop! Let's get to work," Darius said. "Let me get the block and tackle my dad and I made and see if it works." He ran to the garage and returned with the pieces. "We can use this to lift the heavy stuff, but then I'll just put up a simple pulley after."

He guided Joe and Katie as they put the rope through and around the block and tackle ends, then he climbed to the floor of the treehouse to attach one end out over a branch so that it hung down beside the treehouse.

Paulie and his mother returned to the house leaving the others to their work.

They attached one end of the block and tackle to ropes coming off an old pallet Darius borrowed from Mr. Wilson. Then they stacked a few of the boards.

Because the block and tackle was only attached to the pallet ropes at the center, it swung wildly.

"Look out, Katie," yelled Darius from the treehouse. She ducked just in time. It missed her head by inches.

"Sorry about that," said Mr. Wilson. "I should have warned you."

"Now I know why construction workers wear hard hats," Katie said.

"It would be easier if I just carried the boards up the ladder one at a time," Joe paused, "and safer."

"No, this will work, I'm sure of it," Darius argued. He gave the rope a firm tug, but the pallet tipped, and all the boards slid off. "Dang it." He lowered the pallet to the ground.

"I'll carry them up," Joe offered again.

"No. You still have to be careful," Darius insisted. "This will work. We just have to figure out how."

They stopped working and set about finding a solution. Mr. Wilson sat listening to their ideas but kept quiet. Darius had a feeling Mr. Wilson already knew a solution. But he was right. If they figured it out on their own, they'd remember it better.

Joe spoke up. "What if we tied a rope to both ends of the pallet?"

"Wouldn't it still spin at the block and tackle?" Katie asked.

"What if we tied ropes to the ends, and I held them from up on the treehouse?" Darius asked. "I could kind of steer it while Joe pulled it up."

"Or we could each hold one and steer," said Katie.

"Great idea," said Mr. Wilson. "Let's give it a try."

Darius was just about to follow Katie up the treehouse ladder when his mother leaned out the kitchen door.

"Darius, this phone call is for you."

11

BAD NEWS

At dinner that evening, it was just the Knight family.

After the meal, Darius's mother handed his father an envelope. "This came in the mail today addressed to you. It's from the building inspector. I didn't want to spoil our dinner in case it is bad news."

He opened the envelope and read to himself, but reread part of it aloud. "You have thirty days from receipt of this letter to remove the treehouse. A fine will be incurred for non-compliance."

"It sure is bad news," Darius said. "But Mr. Wilson doesn't seem worried about it."

"We should show him this letter and get his opinion," said Darius's father. "Let's invite him over for dessert and coffee. I don't want to wait on this."

"Me neither," said Darius.

Mr. Wilson was glad for the invitation and came right over.

"Who can resist apple pie?" he said.

He read the letter. "Bilgewater up to his tricks again. It just so happens there is a Rocky Point town board meeting in two weeks. I plan on attending. I'd appreciate it if all of you would join me."

"The way you are smiling, Mr. Wilson, makes me think you are up to something," said Darius's mother.

"Me? No. Just being a good citizen." Mr. Wilson winked at Darius. "Great pie, by the way."

Darius told him about the new job they had lined up for Mrs. Baker's friend.

"We have enough wood from the construction site to rebuild her steps, but if we get more jobs, what do we do then?

"It might be time to start keeping track of your expenses and earnings, especially if you have to buy things."

"I can teach them how to set that up," Darius's father said. "Working with income and expenses is what I do at Preston Enterprises. It's a very important part of every business."

***

On Tuesday morning, Darius, Katie, and Joe rode their bikes to the construction site. Now that the treehouse was complete, they decided to keep bringing scrap wood for use in future projects.

When they arrived at the woodpile, Beverly, the

project manager, called down to them from the house and waved for them to come to her.

They hurried up the driveway.

"I was hoping you kids would come by today. Ready for a tour?"

"Yes," the three replied in unison.

Beverly walked them to the front door, opened it, and let them in.

"Wow!" Joe said. "This is huge." He looked around at the two-story entranceway with the brass chandelier hanging from the ceiling. To their left and right were large rooms. In front of them was a wide staircase with a carved handrail. Beverly walked them into the kitchen, explaining where the stove and refrigerator would go and how the cabinets would look. She pointed to the pantry and downstairs bathroom.

"The downstairs is nearly completed. The walls are in, and we're about to call in the paint crew to start while we finish the upstairs. Hold on a minute. I'll be right back." She left the kids and walked out onto a large back deck through a sliding glass door.

Darius walked to the opposite end of the kitchen. "There are more rooms over here."

Beverly returned, handing each of the kids a yellow hard hat. "You'll need these upstairs." Off the kitchen was a set of stairs leading to the second floor. "These are what we call the back stairs."

Workers were putting up pieces of drywall on the wall studs, so the open expanse was becoming separate rooms. Beverly narrated their tour. "Bedroom, bedroom, bathroom, bedroom, office, bathroom, playroom."

"Look at all the wires in the walls," Katie said. "It's like a whole secret world."

Darius had a different focus. "Look at all the different tools."

"It makes our little treehouse look like nothing," Joe said.

Beverly stopped and turned to the kids. "You built a treehouse? That is awesome. Don't ever put yourself down. Everyone has to start somewhere. Most kids your age don't even know how to use a hammer correctly. You should be proud of yourselves."

Joe's cheeks turned a little red. "You are right."

"How much longer until you finish?" Darius asked. What he really wanted to know is how much longer would they have to carry scrap wood home.

"About two weeks, I think, if everything stays on schedule." Beverly ushered them down the front stairs and to the door. They removed their hard hats and handed them to Beverly.

"Thank you so much," Katie said.

"My pleasure," Beverly replied. She turned to Darius. "Would you give me your address? I think we can help you with that wood."

"Sure."

Beverly handed Darius one of her business cards. "Just write your address on the back."

Darius did but took a good look at the front of the card before he returned it.

"Here," Beverly said, handing him a card. "You can have one to keep."

"Thanks."

The three kids walked back down the gravel driveway and loaded up some wood.

"I wish we could have seen the home theater in the basement," Katie said.

"I forgot about that. Maybe Beverly will let us tour again. Then we can ask."

***

"We need a pair of binoculars," said Katie looking out from the treehouse. "The boats on Happy Lake look like specks."

"The white ones look like ducks," replied Joe.

"I know what to ask for my birthday," Darius said. "If my parents haven't bought my gifts already."

"That's right, July fifth. I remember now." Katie stood up and leaned against one of the corner posts of the treehouse. "I won't be older than you anymore."

"You're still two months older no matter what," Darius pointed out. "When's your birthday, Joe?"

"April."

"You're just a year older than me," Katie said.

"But you are eighth graders and I'm a high schooler."

"Well, since we're home-schooled, we're not really in a grade. We work at our own pace," Darius explained.

"Do you get summer off?"

"We can take breaks if we want."

"If our parents let us, he means," added Katie.

"But I like to keep going. I'm hoping to graduate a year early."

"You can do that?"

"Sure."

"Speaking of breaks, are we set to do Mrs. Kotarski's steps Friday morning? I told her I'd let her know today. My dad is buying another couple of boxes of screws. We'll have to pay him back, he said, as a business expense. Wait until I tell you what she said she'd pay us."

"Ten dollars each?" Katie guessed.

"Nope. Fifty dollars for us to split."

"Wow!" said Joe. "But that doesn't split evenly."

"Don't forget, we have to subtract the cost of the screws."

"Still," Katie said, "that's serious cash. And Mr. Wilson thinks we'll get more jobs."

A loud horn blasting from the front of the house interrupted Katie. The three friends climbed down from the treehouse as fast as they could and ran around to the front yard.

A large flatbed truck was backed into the driveway with a pile of scrap wood secured to the deck.

"Where do you want this?" Dennis called, leaning out of the truck's cab.

"Over here," Darius pointed to the neat stack on the side yard.

Dennis and another construction worker stepped down from the truck. "How 'bout you kids give us a hand."

"Sure thing."

The other construction worker, a tall, thin African American man introduced as Calvin, climbed onto the flatbed and handed the boards down to Dennis. He passed them off to the kids who took turns walking the boards to the pile.

In a few minutes, the entire load was off and stacked.

"Thank you so much, Dennis. This would have taken us days," Darius said.

"Helping you helps us. We wanted it gone before the owners get into town tomorrow to have a look at the place."

"I hope they like it as much as we do," Joe said. "It's an amazing house."

"Thanks. We gotta run. Enjoy your wood."

"Wait," said Katie, "before you go, do you want to see what we built?"

"For a minute." The two men followed the kids around the house. Katie pointed to the treehouse on the ridge.

"That is something," Dennis said. "And all from scraps."

"Well, mostly. The posts we got from our neighbor, and we used a lot of screws."

"If you were older, we'd hire you. We're always looking for good carpenters."

"That's a nice compliment," Katie said. "Thanks."

As the two men pulled away, Joe asked his friends, "Are you guys going to the Fireworks at Happy Lake?"

"Wouldn't miss it," Darius answered.

.

12

SPECIAL DAYS

he Fourth of July came, and Katie's family met the Knights at the Happy Lake Park. Joe and his grandparents joined them a while later. The group walked around for a while, bought ice cream cones at the concession stand, and then set out blankets on the grass to prepare for viewing the fireworks.

"This event seems smaller than last year," Katie's stepfather commented.

"I wonder why," mused Darius's mother. "Hopefully, the fireworks will be as spectacular as always."

They were not disappointed. "Impressive as always," said Katie's mother.

Back at the Knight's house, Darius couldn't sleep. Tomorrow was his birthday.

He must have fallen asleep at some point because the next thing he heard was Paulie's voice. "Wake up, sleepyhead. Dad wants you to come downstairs. Now!"

"Okay, okay." Paulie ran out of the room yelling, "He's up! He's up!"

Darius threw on some clothes and hurried barefoot down the stairs. What could be so important this early?

His parents and Paulie were sitting at the dining room table, a stack of presents in the center. They sang "Happy Birthday" as he entered to room.

His father spoke. "I have to work late tonight, so I thought we could celebrate early."

"Except not the cake part," said Paulie, sounding disappointed.

Darius sat and opened each present as Paulie handed them to him: A power drill, drill bits, several boxes of screws, a toolbox with a hammer, screwdrivers, a level, a square, and three kinds of pliers.

"This is awesome."

"I keep hearing you say 'the right tool for the right job' and I thought these would help," his father said.

"I guess I can give Mr. Wilson's drill back now."

"One more," said Paulie.

Darius opened it.

"Binoculars, now we can spy on Happy Lake from the treehouse."

Everyone laughed and started helping themselves to pancakes.

"I invited your friends over for cake later," said Darius's mother. "We'll save a piece for your father."

***

Friday was a scorcher. Darius wiped the sweat from his forehead as he leaned back after securing the last step. "That was a lot of work. Now I see why Mrs. Kotarski is willing to pay so much."

"But this time, there are three of us," Katie pointed out, "so it was more efficient."

Joe began packing the tools into Darius's backpack. Katie put the small scraps of wood into her basket.

Darius walked up the new back steps and knocked on the door.

"Finished already?" Mrs. Kotarski asked.

"Yes, ma'am."

Mrs. Kotarski stepped onto the back porch and walked down the steps. "How wonderful." She walked back up the steps. "Just wonderful. I'll be right back."

She returned with three twenty-dollar bills and handed one to each of the kids. "A little extra for your good work. And here is something for the materials." She handed Darius a ten-dollar bill.

"Thank you so much, Mrs. Kotarski."

"I hate to admit it, but I had called a handyman last year who quoted me such a high price, I couldn't afford it. Don't let me get started on that Community Contracting guy. When Doris, uh—Mrs. Baker, told me about you kids, I hoped it would work out. And it has."

"I'm glad," said Darius.

The kids said their goodbyes and rode back to Darius's house to put away the tools.

They raced to the treehouse and claimed their seats.

"I've made a schedule of jobs we have lined up," said Darius. "I sent it to you in a shared calendar, so check your phone. If you can't make it, we can change times or days, but if at least two of us can go, I think we should stick to the schedule."

"If we are going to keep doing this, we should think of a name for our business," Katie suggested.

"Good idea," Joe said. "What about Builders 'R Us?'"

"That makes us sound like we build houses," Darius said. "We need something that describes what we do."

"Fixer-uppers?" Joe offered.

"Better," said Darius.

"But we do more than just fix-ups," Katie said.

Darius stood up and stretched. "True. We're more like handymen. We do all sorts of little jobs for people."

"I don't like the 'men' part," said Katie. "Why not Handy Kids?"

"That's it. I like it," Darius said.

"Me, too," said Joe. "Handy Kids it is. Handy Kids Carpentry."

"I wanted to tell you," Darius continued, "I was curious about the handyman Mrs. Kotarski mentioned, the Community Contracting person. You'll never guess who it is. A guy named Kevin Bridgewater."

"What? Is he related to you-know-who?" asked Joe.

"I asked Mr. Wilson. He said it was a nephew to you-know-who. Building inspector Bridgewater was never married."

"No surprise there," Katie said.

***

By mid-July, Handy Kids was in demand all over Rocky Point and Happy Lake. Darius's phone pinged as he and Joe sat in the treehouse after finishing another fix-it job.

"Katie's on her way over," said Darius.

Joe was looking through the binoculars at Happy Lake.

"Mr. Wilson sure was right," Darius said. "Those ladies sure do give us a lot of business. And not just those ladies, busy younger people too."

"I know, we've barely had a day off in the last couple of weeks," said Joe. "I'm not complaining. I

love it. And to think I knew nothing about carpentry before this summer."

"I always wonder what else I might like that I don't know about yet. I drive myself crazy sometimes. My dad says to always be open to new experiences. You never know."

"That reminds me, isn't tonight the town board meeting?" Joe asked.

"Yes, and we're going. I'm dying to know what Mr. Wilson is going to say."

"Maybe more fireworks than the Fourth of July,"

Katie joined the two boys in the treehouse. "Did I hear more fireworks?"

"Figuratively speaking," Darius explained. "Mr. Wilson and Mr. Bridgewater at tonight's town board."

"I've never been to a town board meeting," said Katie. "My stepdad says they're usually very boring."

"Usually, but I have a feeling this one won't be."

.

13

FACING THE TOWN BOARD

he Rocky Point town hall meeting room was nearly full when Darius's family arrived. Katie, her mother, and Joe were already seated and waved them over to the chairs they were saving.

Darius looked around for Mr. Wilson, but he didn't see him.

The meeting was called to order by the town supervisor, and everyone stood for the Pledge of Allegiance. The supervisor then sat and proceeded to go through the agenda items.

A half hour went by with reports from various committees, budget requests, and recommendations. All the while, Mr. Bridgewater sat in his seat at the end of the table, not saying a word. Then it was his turn to make his report. He read a list of things he had accomplished that month. Then he took a deep breath and looked right at the Knights.

"It has come to my attention that an illegal structure has been built in our town. The owners were contacted by me and told to remove it, but they refused. They were sent a written statement giving them thirty days to comply, but I have seen no work to remove the structure as yet. I bring this to the board's attention because I fear further action will need to be taken."

The supervisor asked, "Have they been told of the fine they will be charged if the structure is not removed?"

"Of course," replied Bridgewater.

"Then wait until the thirty days is up and send them the bill. If they refuse, we will remove it at their expense. Next item?"

Darius couldn't believe it. Nothing? Standing in the back of the room. Mr. Wilson looked at Darius and gave a thumbs up. Darius had no idea what was happening.

The meeting continued for another fifteen minutes. The supervisor then announced that it was time for public comments.

The supervisor pointed toward the back of the room.

"My name is John Wilson. I live in Hilltop Meadows. I have a question about the illegal structure. By what town ordinance is the structure considered illegal?"

The supervisor looked at Bridgewater.

Bridgewater shuffled his papers. "Section 8, part C, paragraph 2. No structure shall be constructed in the town without prior authorization of the town board

which will issue a permit upon satisfactory inspection of the project plan."

"Seems pretty straightforward," said the supervisor.

Mr. Wilson continued. "And what does the next paragraph, Section 8, part C, paragraph 3 state?"

Bridgewater looked at his paper again.

"Let me help you, Mr. Bridgewater," said Mr. Wilson. "I believe it says an exception to this ordinance would be play structures built by or for children, such as playhouses, forts, treehouses, and similar structures."

"But, but . . ." sputtered Bridgewater. "How are we to know they are safe?"

"I would think the parents have that responsibility."

"Well, I think I should be the one to determine that," said Bridgewater, raising his voice. "After all, I'm the building inspector."

"And let me remind you, I was the building inspector years before you. And furthermore, I was on the committee that wrote those laws which the town board voted on and approved. If you don't like the law, set up a committee and revisit it. I'll gladly volunteer to be on that committee."

A few sniggers could be heard from the crowd.

"I won't be needing your input, Wilson," Bridgewater snapped.

"Admit it, Bilgewater, you just don't like kids."

When Bridgewater heard his old nickname, he tensed and started huffing.

"Let's move on," said the supervisor. "Are there any other comments from the public?"

"I have one." Darius recognized Mr. Hansen. They had built a ramp into his shed a week ago. "I happen to know the builders of that treehouse, and I must say, they are good kids. I even had them build something for me. Not a treehouse. I'm a little old for that." A few chuckles from the crowd interrupted him. "The quality of their work is excellent."

"Thank you, Mr. Hansen," said the supervisor.

The supervisor must know him already, thought Darius. Mr. Hansen never said his name.

"I don't see a building permit for you, Mr. Hansen," said Bridgewater. "Perhaps you have broken the law." His smug gotcha look reminded Darius of what Mr. Wilson said earlier about him always trying to be superior to everyone.

Mr. Hansen looked him in the eyes. "I never said they built a structure."

Several people in the crowd laughed as Bridgewater fumed in his seat.

The meeting ended shortly after that, and Mr. Wilson met the group outside the town hall.

"I was wondering when you were going to say something, Mr. Wilson," Darius said.

"I had to wait until they called for public comment. I had to make sure I followed the rules so they couldn't stop me from speaking."

"I think you made your point," said Darius's father.

"Well, Bilgewater can't make you take down the treehouse, at least."

Mr. Hansen paused as he passed by the group. "Hey kids, keep up the good work." He gave a quick wave and continued on his way.

"Who is that guy?" Katie asked.

Mr. Wilson answered. "Mr. Hansen? He's a Hollywood producer. I've known him for years. When I had my construction business, I built the cabinets for his kitchen."

"I'm guessing he's rich from the fancy house," Katie said.

"Fancy house?" Mr. Wilson replied. "This is just his getaway place. He has a mansion in Los Angeles and a penthouse in New York City. And those are just the ones I know about."

"Wow," said Joe. "How does a person get that rich?"

"I think a combination of hard work and good investments. You guys are already doing the hard work part. That's why when he called me about replacing his shed ramp, I directed him to you three."

They started for their cars in the dimming evening light while Paulie and Katie's younger brothers were chasing each other in circles around the adults. The older three trailed behind. They saw Bridgewater scurrying across the parking lot, clutching his papers. He gave Darius an icy stare, then walked with his nose in the air to his black sedan.

"What was that about?" whispered Katie.

"I wish I knew," Darius whispered back.

.

14

NEW BUSINESS

"I don't think there will be much more scrap wood now that the house is almost finished," Joe said as the three friends stacked the latest load of boards at Darius's house. "I hope that our customers don't mind the extra charges for supplies."

Darius replied, "When my dad was teaching me how to set up a spreadsheet for tracking our income and expenses, he told me that getting a job is not always about the price. Customers want a good price, but he said doing a good quality job on time was just as important. As long as they don't feel overcharged for our quality and time frames, we'll keep getting jobs."

"And more jobs mean more profit. My stepdad says I should look into investing some of my money. I'm not sure what that means yet, but he says it's a way to make your money grow instead of having it sit in a bank account earning very little interest. I'm supposed to talk to his financial advisor sometime."

"My parents have a 401(k). All I know is that it helps them save money for when they retire," said Darius.

"I never heard of any of this," Joe said. "I better get learning about it if I'm earning money. Maybe it will help pay for college."

"Good idea, Joe. And we can all talk to my step-dad someday to learn more about investing. I like the idea of my money making money rather than us working all day," Katie said.

"I vote for a break in the treehouse," Darius said, raising his hand.

"Me, too," Katie and Joe said in unison as they raised their hands. The trio raced to the treehouse and climbed the ladder one by one.

***

After dinner, the doorbell rang. Darius jumped up to answer it, but Paulie beat him to the door.

"Hi," said the stranger, a man that looked about their father's age. Behind him, a red-haired boy about seven years old peeked out from behind his leg. "Is your mother or father home?"

By that time, Mr. Knight was standing behind his sons. "Yes, may I help you?"

"I was passing by, and I noticed the treehouse in your backyard. I was hoping to inquire who built it. I would like something for my kids. Is that something you built, or did you hire it done?"

"Neither. My son and his friends built it."

"Oh." He sounded disappointed. "Thank you, anyway." The man turned to leave.

Darius looked at his father.

"Wait," his father called. "They might be interested in building one for you. They have a little business, mostly small carpentry repairs."

The man's face brightened. "My name is Bob Caswell, and this is my son Shane." He reached out and shook Darius's hand and then his father's. His son did the same. "Maybe we can work something out. I don't actually have a tree, but maybe a playhouse?"

Darius nodded. "I will have to talk with my friends first. We haven't built anything that big for anyone, other than the treehouse for ourselves."

"There's a first time for everything. Talk to your friends. Let me know either way." Mr. Caswell pulled out a business card and handed it to Darius. *Another business card*, noted Darius. "I don't live far, about a quarter mile down Davis Road."

"I will get back to you soon," Darius said, holding up the business card.

They watched the visitors get into their car and drive off.

"Can I build a playhouse?" asked Paulie.

"Let's talk about that as a family," said their father while ushering them back to the living room.

"I heard Mr. Caswell," said their mother. "Your business is growing, Darius. That must be exciting."

"I guess so. There is a lot to think about to build a whole building, even if it's just a playhouse. I'll have to do some Internet searching to find some ideas."

"Make sure it's what your customer wants before you start building," said his father.

"Just getting all the materials there will be a challenge. It's not like we can fit big boards on our bikes."

"You can have things delivered by the lumberyard. Maybe even get Mr. Caswell to pay for them directly. It will be easier for your record-keeping."

"That would be great."

"Think bigger. Talk to Mr. Wilson, too. He had his own business. He'll have some good tips, I'm sure."

"So can I have a playhouse, too?" asked Paulie again.

"Let's make that a family project," said their father. "We can design it together and Darius can show us how to construct it. What do you think, Darius?"

"Sure." Darius also thought that if Paulie had a place of his own, he wouldn't want to be in the treehouse. "Paulie could invite his friends over to play in his own playhouse."

***

The next morning, Darius, Katie, and Joe met Mr. Wilson in his barn workshop.

"You want my advice?" Mr. Wilson asked. "I'm honored." He took a little bow and motioned them to sit down in chairs he had set out. "What would you like to know?"

"Well, my dad helped me set up the bookkeeping to track income and expenses, so I can do that. And I've made a shared calendar so we can schedule jobs. But it's so much to make sure we have everything we need for supplies, and tools, and everything."

"You are realizing that running your own business is a lot of work."

"Yes."

"The first thing you need to ask yourselves is do you want to be your own boss or do you want to work for someone else and have them as a boss. Is the extra work worth the reward?"

"What's the big difference if you are doing the same type of work?" asked Joe.

"If you are your own boss, you get to decide what work, when, and how much. If you work for someone else, you are limited by their decisions. If you are your own boss, the sky's the limit, depending on how much value you can provide to your customers."

"Don't most people work for someone else?" asked Joe.

"Yes, that's true, but people who are self-motivated and who want to achieve big results and be successful are the ones who work for themselves. Eventually, they may be the head of a big company that they started."

"Then they are the other people's boss," Katie said.

"Exactly. Now you have to decide which you want to be."

"My mom always has a boss no matter where she works, and they aren't always very nice. They don't pay her very well either," Joe said.

"My dad has a boss," added Darius, "but he is a boss over other people, so he's kind of in the middle, I think."

"My parents both have bosses," said Katie. "I hear them complaining sometimes."

Mr. Wilson stopped them. "I don't mean to say that having a boss is bad. Some people, most people, prefer it. Tell me what I need to do for my paycheck and I'm fine with it. But you have to decide what's best for you, that's all. I get the feeling you would all rather be bosses."

"If I can get everything together and not worry so much," Darius said.

"The key to that is being organized. You can make a system with checklists for every type of job you do. Then you don't have to remember everything every time. You just follow the system you already wrote. And the more experience you get, the easier it will be to develop a system that works for you."

"Thanks, Mr. Wilson. My dad was right. You have good advice."

"Now, let's look at those playhouse ideas you brought."

They spent the next hour or so discussing the various plans Darius found on the Internet.

***

The three friends ate a quick lunch at Darius's house, then headed out on their bikes to pick up more wood at the new house construction site.

"This might be it," Joe said, "but we've been lucky to get so much."

"Our customers will have to pay more if we have to buy all the wood from now on," Katie said.

"As long as we provide better value than that other guy, we'll keep getting jobs," Darius said as he secured the last of the longer boards to his bike.

"Hey kids," called a voice from the new house. It was Beverly waving at them.

They walked up the long driveway.

"One last look inside?"

"Sure," they agreed.

This time, the rooms had been painted light cream colors, and the fixtures were all attached. The kitchen appliances were in place.

"Is the basement finished?" asked Katie.

Beverly led them down the stairs. She opened a door to the movie theater room with dark walls and a slanted floor. "The reclining theater seats haven't arrived yet, but you get the idea."

They walked through the basement and Beverly pointed out the game room, laundry room, and fitness room. At the other end, they walked up a flight of stairs that opened into the two-car garage.

"I'm afraid to ask what they paid for this," Joe said.

"Be afraid," Beverly chuckled. "Way more than I can afford with this job. I can build it, but I can't afford to live in it."

Darius remembered what Mr. Wilson said about owning a company and being your own boss or having a job and working for someone else. *I think I'd rather be my own boss.*

On their way back to Darius's house, they had to

stop and move to the side of the road with their loads of wood. A black sedan slowed down and then sped past.

"Was that who I think it was?" Joe asked.

"If you were thinking Bridgewater, you were right," Darius answered.

Ethan A. Wohlwend

15

y Saturday morning they had met with Mr. Caswell and his son to find out exactly what they wanted built. After a little time, they agreed on the perfect plans for the playhouse and ordered the materials they needed.

Back home, Paulie asked again but increased his request.

"We're not building a castle, Paulie," said his father. "A playhouse."

"A fort?" asked Paulie.

"Sure, we can call it a fort," Darius said. "We can use the same plans as the Caswell's but make window holes that have shutters that close to keep out the enemy."

"Cool," said Paulie. "Who's the enemy?"

"Use your imagination. Girls with cooties, maybe."

"Eww."

"Using the same plans is a great idea, Darius. No sense reinventing the wheel," said their father.

"What wheel?" asked Paulie. "It has wheels?"

Their father laughed. "No wheels, Paulie. It means making extra work for yourself."

Darius was not sure Paulie understood completely,

but there were more important things to take care of. "Where are we going to build this exactly?"

"I was thinking in the far corner of the backyard, opposite the treehouse."

"Sounds good to me," Darius said.

"Someone's here," Paulie said, jumping up from the sofa. "I heard a car." He ran to the front window, then ran back. He whispered, "It's the police."

Their father walked to the front door. As he reached the door, the doorbell rang.

"How can I help you, officer?" As he asked, he saw another officer walking toward the side of the house and looking back.

"You are William Knight, the owner of this residence."

"Yes."

"We have a report that kids were seen stealing wood from a construction site a short distance from here. They were also observed stopping at this address. My partner has located the wood on the side of your house. Are you aware of this?"

"I'm aware of the wood, yes. That it was stolen? It most certainly was not. My son had permission to take the scrap wood from the project manager."

"And what would his name be?"

Darius's father motioned for him to come to the

door. Darius felt himself shaking. The police had never been to their house before. He knew he had done nothing wrong, but still, he felt guilty.

"Do you know the name of the project manager?" his father asked.

"Her name is Beverly. I don't know her last name."

"You wouldn't know how to contact her, would you?" the officer asked.

Darius shook his head. His eyes were fixed on the officer's equipment, a handgun secured in its holster and a pair of handcuffs hung from his belt.

The officer sighed. "We are going to have to contact her or someone from the company to confirm the story. Don't go anywhere." The officer walked back to the patrol car and sat inside. It looked to Darius that he was talking on the radio.

He and his father stood in the doorway for what seemed like an hour.

"What's happening?" whispered Paulie from behind the door.

"Nothing," Darius whispered back.

The officer walked back to the front door. "My sergeant spoke to the owner of the company. He knows nothing about it. He said there are signs on the fence around the site to keep people out. It looks like theft. He says to prosecute."

Darius swallowed. *This can't be happening.* He felt his hands shaking and hoped the officer couldn't see them. When his father put a hand on his shoulder, he relaxed a little.

"What happens now?" asked Darius's father.

"As the owner of the property where the materials were found and parent of the suspect, you will be issued a summons to court and charges will be levied."

"And if we can straighten this out before then?"

"That's between you and the court."

"Fine."

Darius could tell that his father was holding in his temper. "Sorry, Dad," he said.

"It's not your fault. It's a misunderstanding. The police are just doing their job."

The second officer got out of the car and pulled the first officer aside. He whispered something into his ear.

The first officer returned to the doorway. "My apologies, Mr. Knight. Our sergeant called to say the construction company owner got in touch with the project manager. It seems the kids did have permission. My apologies again. Have a good day."

"Do you mind if I ask who reported to the police?" Darius's father asked.

"That I don't know. You'd have to speak to the sergeant."

"Thank you."

As soon as the officers headed for their car, Darius and his father went inside, closed the door, and sat in the living room.

"Well, that was something!" his father sighed.

"I knew I didn't do anything wrong, but I did get scared."

"I admit, I was a bit concerned that it would become a big thing. I wonder who would report this. You kids have been hauling wood for a month now."

"I bet I know." Darius told his father about Bridgewater passing them on the road the day before.

"I bet you're right. There is a lesson in all of this for you."

Darius thought for a minute. "Get permission in writing if you are taking stuff?"

"That would be great. I was thinking you should at least make sure you have the contact information of the person who gave you permission."

"Oh, no," Darius moaned. He ran up to his room and picked up a business card from his dresser. Right there in bold letters was the name Beverly Bark, Project Manager, with her cell phone number at the bottom. He ran back down the stairs to show his father.

"I can't believe I forgot I had this."

"You were stressed. It's hard to think straight."

"I don't like that kind of stress."

"Trust me. Nobody does." His father laughed.

Paulie called from the front window, "Mom's home."

Everyone went outside to help her with the groceries. Paulie was jumping up and down. "The police were here. The police were here."

Their mother's eyebrows raised. "What did I miss?"

16

A CHANCE MEETING

After making a few small changes in the Caswell playhouse plan, Darius, Paulie, and their parents began building Paulie's fort.

"This is going so much faster than the Caswell's playhouse. It's much easier to build the same thing over again. I'm glad we made that checklist on the first one," said Darius. "Less thinking and more doing."

"I'm glad you are in charge, Darius," said his mother. "I'm not sure what I am doing without getting specific directions."

Their father laughed, "Who would have thought our son would be our boss?"

"Hopefully, he's a kind and considerate boss," their mother added while removing her work gloves.

Darius took the hint. "Break time, everybody."

While they enjoyed lemonade and fruit slices at the picnic table, Joe arrived.

"Help yourself," said Darius, offering the tray of fruit.

"Thanks. Wow, you guys have done a lot of the playhouse already, I see."

"Fort," Paulie corrected him.

"It's a fort," Darius explained. "Much better than a plain old playhouse."

"Gotcha," Joe replied. "What can I do to help?"

The family and Joe resumed working on the fort. A couple of hours later, it was assembled.

"Fort Paulie," Paulie exclaimed. He went inside, closed the door, and opened the shutters. "Private headquarters." He closed the shutters and came back outside. "Can I invite Eric and Rayshawn over?"

"Sure, sweetheart," his mother said. "You can use my phone on the kitchen counter."

Paulie ran off toward the house.

"That's one happy boy," said their father. "Thanks for doing this, Darius."

"Not a problem. I figure if Paulie has his own place, he won't be wanting to be using ours. I love him and all, but–"

"You need your own space," his father said. "I get it. I was a teenager once."

"With a treehouse?" Joe asked.

"No, but I had an attic hideout so my friends wouldn't be pestered by my three younger sisters."

***

After Darius and Joe met Katie at her house, they rode their bikes to the library in Happy Lake.

Joe said, "I've never been to this library before. I just get books from the school library."

"There is a lot more than books in this library," Katie said.

As they passed the community bulletin board in the entryway, a tall, thin, blond-haired teen was tacking up a poster.

"What is a PAV race?" asked Joe, reading the poster.

The teen turned toward them. "PAV sands for Programmable Amphibious Vehicle. We're hosting a competition at the park on Labor Day. You should come."

Darius took a photo of the poster with his phone. "Thanks. Are you in it?"

"No, but my friends and I are running it. I'm Atlas, by the way. Nice to meet you, but I gotta run and put up these posters." He gave a wave and left.

"Do you know who that was?" asked Joe. "He's the kid who got rich from inventing some drone thing. Everybody at school is talking about it. I recognized his name."

"Wait. Is he the same guy who started the drone prescription delivery service for the pharmacy?" Katie asked.

"He is."

"My grandpa loves that service. Medicine right to his door in minutes."

"He sounds like someone I'd like to talk to," Darius said.

They gave Joe a library tour and got him to sign up for a library card. On their way out they decided to stop for ice cream at a shop on Main Street.

"Look, there's that guy, Atlas," said Darius. "I'm going to introduce myself." *What's the worst that can happen?* thought Darius. *He could tell me to get lost.*

Darius walked up to Atlas sitting in a booth by himself. "Hi. We met earlier at the library. My name is Darius. My friend tells me you are an inventor."

"People call me that. I've invented a few things."

"I heard about the drone delivery."

"Not my first invention. I started small. I had a lawn mowing business and had to get my lawn mower to each house, so I used some old stuff to create a cart to pull it."

"That was you? Wow! My friends and I do carpentry work for people, and your cart gave me an idea of how to carry wood and tools."

"That's great."

"My question is, how did you learn to invent things?"

"Like anybody else, I guess. I see a problem, and I try to figure out a way to solve it."

"I wish I could do that."

"Who says you can't? I'm always trying to learn about everything. If I had advice on inventing, I'd say read, read, read. The Internet is your friend. The library is your friend. And never limit your imagination. If you are creative enough and take action you can accomplish anything!"

The waitress brought Atlas's order and placed it on the table.

"Thanks for your help, Atlas," Darius said. "And if you have a few extra fliers, we can hang them around Rocky Point for you."

"That would be great. The bigger the crowd the better." Atlas gave him a stack of fliers and Darius walked back over to join Joe and Katie.

"Well?" asked Joe, "What did you talk about?"

"Inventing. I definitely want to go to the PAV race."

***

"It looks like another letter from the town," said Darius bringing the letter to his father. "I wonder what it's about this time."

His father opened it and read it to himself.

"Good grief," his father said. "Now Bridgewater wants to stop you kids from doing your carpentry jobs."

"Why?"

"It's not very clear. Safety? Ages? It can't be a permit. We already went through that."

"I think I might know. Did you know that Community Contracting, the guy that does carpentry work, is Bridgewater's nephew?"

"Is that so? Maybe it's time we go back to the town board. Let's find out what Mr. Wilson thinks."

***

The kids had a chance to discuss this with Mr. Wilson the very next day. He wanted their help fixing his friend's porch railing.

"This is Bob Kline. We grew up together. I told him I was retired, but he insisted I fix this railing. I told him I had some young helpers." Mr. Wilson winked.

"Nice to meet you young people. Johnny tells me you are learning to be carpenters. That's great. Johnny thinks he's too old." Mr. Kline laughed until he started to cough.

"Nice to meet you, too, Mr. Kline," said Darius. "Mr. Wilson is teaching us."

"Just don't be like that Bilgewater fellah. He came one day and put a few screws in the railing and said, 'good enough.' Can you believe it? The railing was still wobbly. When I called him, he said it was fixed, he wanted his payment. I said it's not done and I'm not giving him anything, because if a job is not all done, it's not done at all."

"Good words to live by, Bob," said Mr. Wilson. "We'll make sure this is all done."

"I'll leave you to it."

After Mr. Kline went back into his house, they filled Mr. Wilson in on the letter from Bridgewater.

"Here we go again," sighed Mr. Wilson.

Darius noticed a hint of a smile. *Mr. Wilson is planning something.*

17

FACE OFF

arius and his family arrived early with Mr. Wilson at the town board meeting. The room filled steadily as meeting time approached. Katie's family and Joe sat near Darius.

"It's packed tonight," said Joe.

Darius looked around. He was surprised to see Mrs. Baker and Mrs. Kotarski. The more he looked, the more he realized that the room was filled with their customers.

"Are you seeing what I'm seeing?" he whispered to Joe and Katie. "We did work for a lot of these people."

"How would they all know to be here?" Katie asked.

"I think Mr. Wilson is up to something again," Darius said in a hushed tone.

"I hope so," replied Joe.

The meeting proceeded much the same as last month's meeting, but no mention was made of the letter sent by Bridgewater.

Public comment was next. Mr. Wilson raised his hand.

"My name is John Wilson. I live in Hilltop Meadows. I have a question for the building inspector."

Bridgewater sat upright and glared at Mr. Wilson.

"I understand that a letter was sent asking certain neighborhood kids to stop doing handyman-type work for their neighbors. Is that correct?"

Bridgewater sputtered out a "Yes."

"As a former building inspector, I don't recall any law prohibiting kids from helping their neighbors. Is there a new law on the books?"

"No, but they are not just helping their neighbors. They are getting paid."

"So, you would like them to work for free? Do you also want babysitters to work for free? Or dog walkers to work for free? Maybe lawn mowers?"

"Mr. Wilson," Bridgewater said, raising his voice, "I know what you are trying to do?"

"And what would that be?"

"Oh, never mind."

"There are a few people who would like to speak if they may. Mrs. Baker?"

"Thank you, Mr. Wilson. I would just like to say those kids did a splendid job repairing my back steps. And they were affordable. The other handyman was too expensive for my limited income."

"The same for me," added Mrs. Kotarski. "I put off repairs because they were too expensive with the other guy."

A chorus of other voices agreed.

Mr. Wilson continued. "Now who is this other guy these ladies are talking about? Any ideas, Bilgewater?"

Bridgewater glared at Mr. Wilson with pursed lips and breath held.

"It's none other than your nephew, isn't it? Then it occurred to me. Why would you want to stop these kids from doing handyman repair? Oh, could it be too much competition for your nephew? Why, Bilgewater, that's un-American. And from an elected official. Shame on you."

"I'm not voting for him again," someone in the crowd said. That comment was followed by much murmuring and head shaking.

The supervisor leaned forward. "I think the board would approve of the kids continuing with their work. I will speak with Mr. Bilge—I mean Bridgewater privately. Thank you all for coming."

Outside, the group stood on the sidewalk next to the parking lot.

"That was good, Mr. Wilson," said Darius.

"Very dramatic," his mother added.

"I'll admit. I had some help. Mr. Hansen, my movie producer friend, gave me some pointers to give my speech some punch."

"It worked," said Darius. "We get to keep our

business. Speaking of which, I have something for everyone. He pulled a small box out of his pocket and handed everyone a business card.

"Handy Kids Carpentry, Darius, Katie, and Joe, with your phone number. Very nice," said Katie's mother.

"And the hammer and saw is a nice touch," Mr. Wilson added.

"I bought them as a surprise, but I was afraid to show them after we got that letter. Now we can pass them out everywhere. I have a box of a thousand," said Darius.

"We'll be busy for years," Joe said, "but I'm not complaining."

***

Labor Day arrived. Katie called Darius. "I have to bring Lionel to the park with me. "He's almost twelve, but you wouldn't know it by the way he acts."

"I could bring Paulie, and they could hang out together," Darius offered.

"That would be great," Katie said. "Thank you. We'll see you there. My parents are dropping us off at the park entrance."

"My dad is going to bring Joe and me down. And Paulie, too. My parents are coming later."

From over Darius's shoulder, Joe asked, "Are we bringing business cards to pass out?"

"Good idea." Darius hung up his phone and ran upstairs to his room to get the cards.

***

Once the friends and brothers gathered downtown, they decided to walk around and check out the booths. Paulie and Lionel spent most of their money on the games of chance, but Darius had other things on his mind.

"I think the PAV race is over there," Joe said, pointing to the other end of the park where a large group gathered.

"It's almost time," said Darius. He scanned the crowd, hoping to see Atlas. He should be easy to spot being so tall—if only I wasn't so short.

Darius was in luck. Atlas stood on a table with a microphone, addressing the huge crowd.

The race began, and people moved toward the ropes to see the machines race out onto the lake and back again. Darius, Katie, and Joe managed to get to a spot where they could see quite well.

"This is awesome," Joe shouted.

After an hour or so, the races ended, and the winners were announced. Darius wanted to talk to

Atlas, but he was always busy. At one point, Atlas saw him and waved, but then he lined up for photos.

Katie's brother, Lionel, insisted on ice cream, and the group decided it would be a good time to find a place to sit and have a treat. Darius still hoped to talk with Atlas, but he was nowhere around.

***

Later that day, they gathered at the treehouse. "I won't be able to do as much work now that football practice has started," Joe said. "Between that and school, I think I'll only be able to work on weekends, and that's only when we don't have games." He stood up from his folding chair and leaned on the treehouse railing.

"Don't worry," Darius assured him, "Katie and I have plenty of schoolwork, too. And I will be camping some weekends with the Scouts. I'm sure our future customers will understand."

"They could always hire Bridgewater's nephew if they are in a hurry to get a job done," Katie added.

"As long as they are willing to pay his prices," Darius said. "I'm sure he's glad we're busy with schoolwork."

Katie raised the binoculars and scanned Happy Lake in the distance. "Still nothing."

"What are you looking for?" asked Joe.

"I was hoping to see a drone, but every time I think I see one, it's just a big black crow."

Darius's phone chirped. "Hello?"

"Is this Darius or Joe," the male voice asked.

"It's Darius."

"This is Atlas. We met at the library. And thanks for coming to the races."

"They were great. I'm putting you on speaker. Joe and Katie are right here."

"The reason I'm calling is to ask if you and your friends would be willing to help out with the park fix-ups that we're doing. We're trying to get as many volunteers as possible to repair things and install new playground equipment."

"Wait, you're in charge of the park project? My scout troop has volunteered to help out, too. And I'll bring my carpentry tools."

"I'll help," Katie said.

"Me, too," added Joe.

"Great. I'll let you know the details as soon as we iron a few things out. Can I text this number?"

"Sure. Can I ask how you got my number?"

"One of you gave a business card to my dad at the park."

"It's good to know they work," Darius said.

"They sure do. Nice talking to you. See you at the park."

Darius ended the call and looked at his friends. "It's volunteer, but so what. It's for a good cause."

"Not everything has to be about money," Katie said.

Joe sat back down. "Easy to say when you can pay the bills. If you can't, then everything is about money."

"My stepdad says money is just a tool, and you need to learn how to use it, just like any other tool."

"Then I think I need someone to teach me how to use the money tool," said Joe. "I learned football from my football coach. I need a money coach."

A loud banging came from below. They looked down to see Paulie and his friend Rayshawn closing the shutters on Paulie's fort.

"The cooties are coming! The cooties are coming!" yelled Paulie. "Lock the doors and windows."

"Prepare for battle," Rayshawn yelled even louder.

Darius, Katie, and Joe couldn't help but laugh.

"It's my fault," confessed Darius, "I mentioned cooties the other day."

18

Mr. Wilson volunteered to drive Darius down to the park in his pickup. They loaded his power tools and sawhorses in the back. Katie and Joe were already at the park when they arrived.

Darius was not prepared for the size of the workforce. Not only was his scout troop there, but teens from Happy Lake High School and many adults. There were two trucks from a garden supply store, one piled high with bags of mulch and the other with apple and pear tree saplings and an assortment of small bushes. A dump truck with a load of gravel sat at the edge of the parking lot.

Atlas was busy distributing copies of the park improvement plan to make sure the work went smoothly. A new walkway had been marked out for the gravel and there were labeled posts for each of the fruit trees and bushes.

"I have a list of tasks on this board," announced Atlas to the crowd, "Please choose one that you are most comfortable with, and we can get started."

Darius and Mr. Wilson decided to make repairs to the concession stand.

"I wrote down all our names on the board," said Darius to Joe and Katie.

At the concession stand, they found a stack of boards and nails.

"Did you know Atlas paid for all of this himself?" Joe asked.

"Really?" Katie asked.

"Well, partly with money he raised from the races we watched on Labor Day, but the rest was his."

Darius sighed. "It's not that I'm jealous, but I wish I were him sometimes."

"Because he's tall?" Joe joked.

"Well, now that you mention it. No, seriously, he's such a cool inventor."

Mr. Wilson stopped measuring and turned to them. "Everybody has a skill set that suits them. That guy, Atlas, has a skill set that few people have. He's been able to use his skills to become successful. I'll admit, very successful. But you have a skill set, too. How many kids your age have your carpentry skills? And how many have made a business out of those skills?"

"Around here, just us," Joe answered.

"And you three have made a success of it. Look at all your happy customers," Mr. Wilson said. "You've done a lot of good for your community."

Darius had to admit they had.

After a couple of hours, they finished all the repairs to the concession stand exterior.

"Now for the paint," a voice from behind them said. "This is first-class work."

They turned around.

"Hi, Atlas," Darius said. *A compliment from Atlas! Awesome.*

Darius introduced Mr. Wilson, Katie, and Joe.

"I'm glad to see so many young people take an interest in their communities," Mr. Wilson said. "It makes an old man feel good about the future."

"And hopefully, people of all ages will come to enjoy the new and improved park," Atlas said, holding out his arm. "We have new playground equipment for the kids and a walking trail with benches for everyone."

"As long as my dog is welcome, I will be sure to visit."

"That reminds me," said Atlas, looking over his shoulder. "I need to make sure the trash bins are put along the trail. Thanks for the reminder, Mr. Wilson."

"You're welcome."

Atlas ran off toward a group of teens with shovels trying to read the park map.

"I wonder why he thanked you for the reminder. You didn't even know about the trash cans," Katie said.

"I suspect he has a lot on his mind. And it always pays to be extra courteous. Business lesson number one." Mr. Wilson opened a can of bright white paint. "How do you know a building is cold?" He held up a paintbrush. "Because it needs two coats."

Darius slapped himself on the forehead. "Oh, no, Mr. Wilson. Don't tell that one to my dad. I hear enough dad jokes already."

"I get stepdad jokes. They are just as bad," said Katie.

"I'm lucky then, I guess," said Joe. "No dad, no dad jokes."

Mr. Wilson looked at Joe. "I didn't know that, Joe."

"It happens," Joe said and shrugged it off.

Mr. Wilson lightened the mood. "Now I'll have to make sure to tell lots of jokes whenever you're around. I've got millions of them."

"No," all three kids yelled.

"Maybe you guys would want to see me play football. We have a game on Tuesday at four. It's a home game at Rocky Point."

"I've never been to a high school football game," Darius admitted. "Just watched pro games on TV.

"I've never been either," said Katie. "It will be a new experience."

"Mr. Wilson?" Joe asked.

"A football game? I used to be a quarterback a long time ago."

"There's a lot we don't know about you, Mr. Wilson," Joe said. "Were you good?"

"Let's just say I was better than Bilgewater."

They all laughed. Darius tried to picture lanky, balding Bridgewater playing football.

***

"This is exciting, isn't it, Darius?" Katie asked, zipping up her jacket to ward off the cool breeze.

"The game hasn't even started yet. Luckily, we got good seats. I would have thought there would be more people."

"Joe said they always win against this team, so people think it's boring to watch."

"I read up on the rules, so I'd know what's going on. High School football isn't much different than pro games."

"I just hope Joe doesn't get injured. That's his big fear," Katie added, "And mine, too."

When the teams came onto the field, a cheer went up, and the cheerleaders waved their pompoms on the sidelines.

"How can we tell which one is Joe with those helmets on?" Katie asked.

"He's number thirteen," said Darius, pointing him out.

"Thirteen? You've got to be kidding."

"Luckily, he's not the superstitious type."

They watched the game progress. By halftime, Rocky Point scored three touchdowns, and their rival team scored none.

"I see what they mean," Katie said. "I kind of feel bad for the other team."

"Let's get some hot chocolate."

As the third quarter began, Number thirteen ran to block an opposing player. They both went down, and the ref blew the whistle.

"Oh, no!" yelled Katie. "That's Joe. He's injured."

The medic rushed to the downed players. Darius and Katie watched with their breath held.

Two medics brought a stretcher onto the field. Joe stood up and waved to the bleachers while the other player was lifted onto the stretcher.

"Whew," said Katie, breathing a sigh of relief. "But now I really feel bad for the other team."

"It's football. It has risks. Most things in life do. You have to decide if your goal is worth the risk."

"I guess it depends on what you think is important."

"Yup."

The game ended. Darius and Katie waited for Joe

to come out of the locker room all showered wearing jeans and a Rocky Point hoodie.

"I told you they were easy to beat," Joe said. "I'm hungry. Let's get some burgers."

The three friends walked to The Rocky Point Diner, sat in a corner booth and ordered. While they waited, Joe told them about the football strategies and plays they used in the game.

"Mr. Wilson is right, Joe. Everyone has a skill set, and you have a football skill set that I am clueless about," Darius said. "Impressive."

Katie sat down her water glass and motioned with her chin for Joe and Darius to look across the room. A large, black-haired man in a red jacket sat with his back toward them. Printed on the back of his jacket in bold yellow lettering were the words Community Contracting.

"Do you think that's Bridgewater's nephew?" Katie whispered.

Before either could answer, Bridgewater walked up and sat opposite the man at his table. He picked up his menu and began to scan the choices. Darius, Katie, and Joe were all watching and didn't have time to react when Bridgewater looked directly at them over the top of his menu.

Darius and Bridgewater locked eyes. Bridgewater sneered and looked back at his menu.

"This is awkward," said Darius.

"I just lost my appetite," said Katie.

"Not me," said Joe. "I'm too hungry."

The waitress brought out their orders, and Katie got her appetite back. They kept conversation to a minimum, not wanting to be overheard.

"When we leave, we have to walk right past them," Katie pointed out.

"What are they going to do, trip us?" Joe asked.

"I guess not."

"I'm texting my dad to pick us up here and not at the school. I'll tell him to come inside." Darius pulled out his phone.

"Good idea. You-know-who wouldn't bother us with adults around," Katie said.

"We hope," Joe agreed, popping another French fry into his mouth.

19

ESCAPE

arius's father arrived minutes later and joined them in the booth. "Your text had me a little worried. Why did I need to come inside?"

"Don't look now," Darius explained, "but Bridgewater and his nephew, the carpenter guy, are sitting two tables away."

"Are they bothering you?"

"No, but Bridgewater gave me a nasty look." Darius glanced in Bridgewater's direction. "He's looking at us now."

"You've done nothing wrong. There is nothing he can do except make faces, so let him."

"When you put it that way, Mr. Knight, it makes him seem silly," Katie said.

"Exactly. Try not to let him bother you. Let me pay for your meals, then we can get out of here." He walked to the front of the diner and waited for the cashier to finish with another customer.

Katie popped the last French fry into her mouth, and the kids stood to leave. Joe led the way, but just before he got to Bridgewater's table, the nephew stood up, faced him, and blocked his way.

"Excuse me," said Joe. Even though Joe was big for his age, he was smaller and shorter than Bridgewater's nephew. Darius noticed the smirk on Bridgewater's face as this was happening.

Joe tried stepping around but was blocked again. "Excuse me," he repeated.

By this point, other patrons near the back of the diner were watching.

"Hey, Community Contracting guy, sit down. Stop being a bully," a voice called.

"Picking on kids? Really?" a woman asked.

"Community Contracting? Is that your business?" someone asked. "I wouldn't hire you after seeing this."

"Me neither," someone else added. "Ridiculous."

Darius thought the guy must have realized he was wearing his work jacket advertising his company on the back because he sat down quickly. Bridgewater sneered at each of the kids as they passed. Darius's father walked back to Bridgewater's table and stood looking at the two men without speaking. Then he turned and followed the kids to the door.

Outside, Joe said his goodbyes.

"I'll give you a ride home, Joe," said Darius's father. "Just to be safe."

Joe laughed. "Thanks, but I live right there." He

pointed to a three-story brick apartment building across the street.

Darius wondered how different his life must be, living in a small apartment and spending so much time alone while his mother worked two jobs. *On the other hand, no lawn to mow, not much to clean up, and a diner across the street.*

***

On Saturday afternoon, the three friends sat in the treehouse, looking out over the valley. The autumn breeze carried the early falling leaves.

"This is my favorite time of the year," Katie announced, "except for the cold part."

Joe took his gaze from the binoculars and looked at Katie. "That doesn't make sense. The cold is a big part of the season."

"But everything else makes up for that," she explained. "That's how I look at it."

"That's how I look at peas," Darius explained. "It's a good meal if I like everything except the peas."

"Hey, guys," Joe said. "I see one. I see a drone. Finally." He handed the binoculars to Katie and pointed.

"I see it. Maybe it's headed to my grandpa's house."

By the time Darius had a turn with the binoculars the drone was gone. "Okay, who wants to get sick so we can order medicine with the drone?"

"I don't think you need to be sick to order something. We should check on that," Katie said, "but I'll bet you need a credit card."

"Remember when Mr. Resnick wanted to pay us with a credit card? We should check into how to do that. I saw a guy at one of the Labor Day booths use something attached to his phone. It looked easy."

"I saw him, too," said Joe. "It took a few seconds."

"Anything to save time," said Katie. "We could be very busy in the spring."

"Let's hope," said Joe. "I could use the money."

"Did you open a bank account?" asked Darius.

"Yes, I wanted to make sure my money wasn't easy to get to and spend. Half goes into the bank. The other half is for me and to help my mom with the bills."

Darius realized how lucky he was to not have to use his money for his family. "I'm sure your mom is glad for the help."

"One thing I'm sure of. I want to earn enough money at one job so that I don't need two jobs to get by. Or like Mr. Wilson says, I could own my own company and be my own boss and the sky's the limit."

"I think we all want that," Katie said. "I'm not sure."

"Hey, you guys," came Paulie's voice from below. "Pull up the bucket. Mom sent you something."

"What?" Darius asked.

"A surprise."

Darius pulled on the rope attached to the pulley and slowly the bucket rose. He grabbed the bucket and pulled it onto the treehouse.

"I can already tell it's cookies by the smell," Darius said. "Thanks, Paulie," he called down.

Paulie ran back into the house. The three friends shared the warm, out-of-the-oven, chocolate-chip cookies.

"Baking cookies. There is a skill I want to learn," said Katie.

"As long as you share," said Joe.

***

With schoolwork to keep the kids busy and the cooler weather keeping people indoors more, the job calls slowed. Although, a few people asked to be placed on their work schedule for the spring and summer.

Mr. Neville was an exception. He wanted the work done right away.

"Of course we will, Mr. Neville," Darius assured him. "This weekend would work for us."

Darius let his friends know of their latest job. "Mr. Neville backed his car into his deck steps. He wants them repaired before his wife gets back from her sister's place in Montana."

"At least we are good with steps," Joe said. "No problem."

"Do you realize how much we sound like professionals?" Katie asked.

"Experience, I think," said Darius. "We know what we are doing now."

"Thanks mostly to Mr. Wilson," Joe said. "I like him a lot. Even the dad jokes, but don't tell him that."

"Speaking of Mr. Wilson, his birthday is coming up," Darius said. "I asked my mom if we could bake him a cake since he lives alone and wouldn't bake one for himself. She said we should throw him a party for all the help he's given us with our business."

"Great idea," Katie said. "When is it?"

"Sunday."

20

PARTY TIME

"It was so nice of you to offer to host this party, Mr. Hansen. You have such a lovely home, perfect for entertaining," said Darius's mother as the family brought in bags of party supplies.

"Why, thank you. When you called, I thought how wonderful. John has done so much for me over the years, it's my gift to him. He has no idea about the party. He thinks he's been asked over to look at some bookshelves I recently purchased."

Darius and Paulie were given the task of blowing up balloons with an air pump, though Paulie seemed to have a hard time not letting go of them so he could watch them fly around the room.

Katie's family arrived a short time later, followed by Joe and his mom. Mrs. Baker brought a cherry pie. Mr. Kline brought his dog so Champ would have a playmate.

"It's almost one, everybody. Are we ready?" asked Mr. Hansen.

Everyone got quiet as Mr. Wilson's pickup pulled into the driveway.

There was a knock on the door.

"Surprise," everyone yelled as Mr. Hansen opened the door. "Happy birthday!"

Darius had never seen a smile so wide on Mr. Wilson's face. They ushered him to the dining room table and sat him in front of the large chocolate cake.

"It only has one candle," Mr. Hansen explained, "because I wasn't sure how old you are."

"It will be easy to get my wish then," Mr. Wilson said and blew out the candle.

Everyone clapped and cheered.

Mrs. Baker put herself in charge of cutting the cake and offering her cherry pie. People helped themselves to the vegetables and dip, chips, and soda.

"I haven't had a birthday like this in years," Mr. Wilson said.

Darius spoke up. "It's also a thank you party, Mr. Wilson, for teaching us about carpentry."

"And business," Joe added.

"And teamwork," said Katie.

"Speaking of business," Darius began, "I brought some business cards if anyone would like one."

"Give me a half a dozen," Mr. Hansen said. "I know people."

Mr. Wilson looked at the business card and cleared his throat. "I'm glad you young people have been

able to learn a set of skills that will help you in the future. It doesn't matter what business you end up in, whether it's carpentry or something else, if you learn the skills of running a business, you can apply them to just about anything."

"So true," said Mr. Hansen. "I didn't start out as a movie producer. I trained to be a dentist."

The room went silent.

"Really?" asked Paulie. "I have a loose tooth."

"Life is full of twists and turns, and here I am today, a movie producer."

"Well, all I can say," began Mr. Wilson, "Darius, Katie, and Joe, thank you for making an old man feel young again."

***

After the party, Katie and Joe came home with Darius. They climbed up to the treehouse and let the rays of the afternoon sun warm them. Katie also wrapped herself completely in a blanket.

"It's getting too cold to be up here very long," Darius noted.

"I say we build walls and install a heater," Joe said.

"Maybe next year."

Joe sat next to Darius. "Your dad asked me what

career I am interested in. I really haven't thought about it much, but he said if I like building things and I'm good at math, I might think about being an architect. I'll have to check that out."

"I have no idea what I'll end up doing," Darius said, "But it will be something I enjoy doing, that's for sure."

Katie uncovered her head. "I want to be a movie producer."

"Really," Joe asked.

"I'd rather be that than a dentist."

Darius stood. "Hey, remember where all of this started? We wanted to build a treehouse. We did. Then we wanted to help Mrs. Baker with her broken steps. We did. We decided to start a business. We did."

"Where is this going?" Katie asked.

"Well, Katie, before that, there was another carpentry project that you mentioned. One that you claimed I didn't really do. Well, now I can say I've done it."

Darius lifted a blanket from under his chair and revealed his project.

"A birdhouse," exclaimed Katie. "I remember now from when we were little."

"That's right. Only this time, I built it all by myself."

Ethan A. Wohlwend

Joe smiled, "When I met you two at the beginning of the summer I never thought I would have been able to do all these things. I never even considered that I could make money anyway other than having a job—or that it could be fun while we were earning money. What do you think we should do next?"

Katie thought that they should learn about investing so their money could make money while they were all at school or playing in the treehouse. "What do you think we should do next Darius?"

Darius gave a mischievous grin. "I have an idea..."

About the Author

Ethan A. Wohlwend started investing when he was five years old and has been buying real estate since he was seven. He graduated with his Ohio Professional Housing Providers certification in November 2019 at just nine years old! That made him the youngest graduate ever, and one of only two minors to ever graduate.

Ethan is currently twelve years old and in 9th grade. He started a real estate business when he was seven that now owns thirty-eight units and is constantly growing. He invests in real estate, gold, silver, and cryptocurrencies. He has spoken in many states all over the Eastern part of the US, and has a goal of speaking in person, in different countries.

At eleven years old Ethan became one of the three lead instructors of the Youth Academy at the National Real Estate Summit. He has been on multiple podcasts, including being interviewed by Rich-Dad Latino and The Real Estate Guys. His podcasts have been heard all over the world. He especially likes seeing and making new friends at conferences.

For fun Ethan loves to drive things. He frequently helps fly the family plane to each of their speaking engagements. He says he will be able to land as soon as he can see over the dashboard. While at home he likes to ride ATVs on the family farm and orchard. He is also frequently found building things out of wood. He is home-schooled, or more accurately vacation-schooled, with his older brother, Deven.

Ethan A. Wohlwend
Clear Sky Training, Ltd.
Speaker, Investor, Author, OPHP, CPL

OTHER BOOKS FROM OUR FAMILY:

Like the lessons taught in this book? Discover the secrets this author learned growing up directly from his parents in *Family Success Triangle*. This book reveals the real life stories and experiences of how the entire family was integrated into business and investing at a very young age.

By Eric M. and Lila J. Wohlwend

"The definitive book on...creating more time freedom, social freedom, and financial freedom."
— Mark Victor Hansen

Look for other books from our family that use fictional characters to teach the same lessons from a kid's point of view. In *The Garage* series Atlas Gold invents new ways of solving problems . . . despite meddling by the mayor, who wants things to stay as they are.

By Deven J. Wohlwend

Please Join My Fruit Tree Challenge

One of the inspirations for this book is my treehouse. My brother and I have always had a treehouse. I am constantly climbing trees. I love to play in trees, and I really love the fruit we get to eat from them. A few years ago, my family and I planted an orchard. Now more and more trees are giving us fruit!

My challenge to you is to plant three or more fruit trees. You can plant them in your backyard or, if you get permission, in your local park. If you just plant three fruit trees, and then challenge your friends to plant three trees, together we can plant millions of trees. With the help of you, the reader, we can make a sequel to the popular YouTuber MrBeast's "Team Trees" - this time with fruit trees.

If everyone who reads this book plants three fruit trees of any kind, they can enjoy the shade to relax and play in. Their family will have fresh fruit every year and if they grow more fruit than they want or need, they can share it with their neighbors. Just like Darius, Katie and Joe are doing, you will make your neighborhood a better place.

Note: The top five easiest fruit trees to grow are:
1. Apple, 2. Pear, 3. Mulberry, 4. Cherry, 5. Peach

Learn more about the family @RealPowerFamily on Instagram, Rumble, and YouTube,
www.ClearSkyTrainer.com